Georgiana Fullerton

Too Strange Not To Be True

A Tale

Georgiana Fullerton

Too Strange Not To Be True
A Tale

ISBN/EAN: 9783741186240

Manufactured in Europe, USA, Canada, Australia, Japa

Cover: Foto ©Andreas Hilbeck / pixelio.de

Manufactured and distributed by brebook publishing software
(www.brebook.com)

Georgiana Fullerton

Too Strange Not To Be True

TOO STRANGE NOT TO BE TRUE.

A TALE.

BY

LADY GEORGIANA FULLERTON,

AUTHORESS OF
'ELLEN MIDDLETON,' 'LADYBIRD,' ETC.

IN THREE VOLUMES.

VOL. II.

LONDON:

RICHARD BENTLEY, NEW BURLINGTON STREET.

1864.

The right of translation is reserved.

TOO STRANGE NOT TO BE TRUE.

PART I.—*Continued.*

CHAPTER IX.

All was ended now; the joy, and the fear, and the sorrow;
All the aching of heart, the restless unsatisfied longing;
All the dull deep pain and constant anguish of patience.
                                                    Longfellow.

   As are our hearts, our way is one,
   And cannot be divided. Strong affection
   Contends with all things, and o'ercometh all things.
   Will I not live with thee ? Will I not cheer thee ?
   Wouldst thou be lonely then ? Wouldst thou be sad ?
                                                    Joanna Baillie.

AT last, one morning, the rain ceased; the heavy clouds rolled away towards the West, and hung in heavy masses over the distant hills; the birds began to sing; the hares and rabbits emerged from their holes, and ran once more over the greensward. The buffaloes came trooping down from the mountains to the prairies, and a hoary bison swam across the river, and looked out upon the

world from one of the flowery islands on its
bosom, like a conqueror taking possession of
a kingdom. A burst of glorious sunshine
gladdened the expanse of wood and water
around St. Agathe, and the herbage and the
flowers, and living things without number,
seemed to exult in its light. The brightness
of that first fine morning, after weeks of in-
cessant rain, was like the first return of joy
to a heart long oppressed by grief. It felt
almost like a presage of approaching change
in the lives of its inhabitants. It was a
Sunday morning, too, and d'Auban, who
heard that Madame de Moldau had been
longing to get to church, brought his horse
ready saddled for her to the door of the
pavilion, and prepared to conduct her in this
way to the village. She consented ; he took
the bridle in his hand, and the Indian servant and the Negro boy followed them on
foot. They crossed the wood between them
and the river, which was sometimes traversed
in a boat and sometimes by means of a series
of small islets forming a kind of natural
bridge, the spaces between being filled up
with a network of floating verdure. Their

progress was slow, for the ground, saturated with wet, was in some places almost impassable. D'Auban kept a little in advance of the horse, and tried at each step the firmness of their footing. The dripping branches over their heads rained upon them as they went along. But the scents were delicious, and the air very reviving to those who had been long confined within the house. For the first time for many weeks Madame de Moldau was in good spirits: she murmured the first words of the service of the Mass— ' I shall go to the altar of God, of God who renews my youth,' and a sort of youthful happiness beamed in her face; she made nosegays of the wild flowers which her attendants plucked for her, from the banks and from the boughs through which they threaded their way. But the flowers were not to adorn the altar, nor the little party, on its way to the church, to hear Mass that day. The sound of the gong, which served as a bell, came booming over the water, but its summons was to sound in vain for them; they were about to be stopped on their road.

D'Auban was just examining whether it

would be possible to cross the river on the island bridge, or to get the boat, when a cry reached their ears—a low, feeble, and yet piercing cry.

'Did you hear?' they all exclaimed at the same time. The boy shuddered, and said it was one of the water-spirits that had cried out. The Indian shaded her eyes with her hand, and with the long-sightedness common amongst her race, discerned a speck in the distance, which she declared was a boat.

'But it is a phantom boat!' she added. 'There is no one in it, and it is coming towards us very slowly ; but it advances, and against the stream.' Madame de Moldau turned pale. She was prone to believe in the marvellous, and easily credited stories of ghosts and apparitions. They all gazed curiously, and then anxiously, at the little boat as it approached.

'There is somebody in it, after all!' the Indian exclaimed.

'Of course there is,' said d'Auban, with a smile ; ' but it is a child, I think ; a small creature, quite alone.'

'It is Simonette,' cried the Indian. 'Good

God! I believe it is.' There was an instant of breathless silence; the eyes of all were fixed on the little boat. It ceased to advance. The oars, which could now be seen, fell with a splash into the water, and the figure of the rower disappeared.

'She has fainted!' cried d'Auban, dreadfully agitated; thought upon thought, conjecture on conjecture, crossing his mind with lightning rapidity. He hastily assisted Madame de Moldau to dismount, made her sit down on a fallen tree, gave his horse in charge to the boy, and then springing from one islet to another, and lastly swimming to the one against which the boat had drifted, he saw the lifeless form of the young girl lying at the bottom of it. There was not a shadow of colour in her face; her hands were transparently thin, and sadly bruised within by the pressure of the oars; a dark rim under her eyes indicated starvation. If not dead, she was apparently dying. D'Auban's chest heaved, and a mist rose before his eyes. It was dreadful thus to see the creature whom he had known from a child, so full of life and spirits, to think of her dying without telling where she had been, what she had done, without hearing words of pardon, blessing and peace. He raised her in his arms, chafed her hands, and tried to force into her mouth some drops of brandy from his flask. After a while she languidly opened her eyes, and when she saw him, a faint smile for an instant lighted up her face. She pointed to her breast, but the gleam of consciousness soon passed away, and she fell back again in a swoon.

He hesitated a moment. Then quietly laying her down again, with her head supported by a plank, he seized the oars, and vigorously pulled towards the spot where Madame de Moldau and the servants were waiting. After a rapid consultation, it was determined that he should row her and the dying girl to the opposite shore, and then return to convey the horse across. The two servants in the meantime contrived to cross the islet bridge. When they met on the other side, the boy was sent to the village to fetch assistance, in order that Simonette might be conveyed to Thérèse's hut, the nearest resting-place at hand, and to beg Father

Maret to come to them as soon as possible. Madame de Moldau had thrown her cloak on some moss less saturated with wet than the long grass, and sitting down upon it, received in her arms the light form which d'Auban carefully lifted out of the boat. She pressed the wasted limbs against her bosom, striving thus to restore warmth to them. She breathed through the cold lips, whilst he chafed the icy feet. They scarcely spoke at all during these moments of anxious watching. Madame de Moldau's tears fell on the poor girl's brow and cheeks. He gazed upon her with the most mournful feelings. Their thoughts were doubtless the same. They wondered where she had been. They prayed she might not die before the priest came.

After swallowing some more brandy, which they had poured down her throat, she revived again a little. D'Auban forced into her mouth some crumbs from a piece of bread he had in his pocket, and in an authoritative manner bade her eat them. She opened her eyes, which looked unnaturally large, and obeyed. After two or three ineffectual attempts at speaking, she succeeded

in saying, as she pointed again to her breast,
'Here, here, in my dress.' To quiet her he
nodded assent, and said he understood; upon
which she closed her eyes again. He went
on putting in her mouth a crumb of bread
at a time.

In the meantime four men from the village
were bringing a sort of rude litter, made of
planks and moss; and Father Maret accompanied them. The boy had arrived at the
church just as he was finishing Mass.

'She has revived a little,' whispered
d'Auban, 'but is scarcely conscious. Feel
her pulse. Will you try and speak to her
now, or can we venture to carry her at once
to Thérèse's hut?'

'I think you may,' said the priest, counting
the beats of her feeble pulse; 'I fear she
will not recover, but there is still some
strength in the poor child. She will be much
more conscious, I expect, in a little while
than she is now.' He drew his hand across
his eyes, and sighed deeply. 'If you please,
I will ride your horse by the side of the
litter, and watch her closely. Wait, however,
for one instant.' Before Simonette was lifted

from Madame de Moldau's knees he bent down and whispered : 'My child, are you truly sorry for all your sins against the good God who loves you so much?'

She opened her eyes, and answered distinctly, 'Yes, Father, very sorry.'

'Then I will give you absolution, my child,' he said, and pronounced the words which have spoken peace to so many contrite hearts since the day that our Lord said, 'Whose sins you shall forgive they are forgiven. Lo, I am with you always to the end of the world.'

After she was laid on the couch of moss, covered with skins, which was Thérèse's bed, Simonette fell fast asleep for two or three hours. When she awoke she eagerly asked for d'Auban and Madame de Moldau.

'Will you not first see the chief of prayer?' said Thérèse, who feared she would exhaust all her strength in speaking to them.

'No! I must see them first; but I wish the Father to come in also.'

In a few moments Madame de Moldau was sitting on one side of her, and Father Maret on the other side of the couch. D'Auban was standing at its foot, more deeply affected

than any one would have thought from the
stern composure of his countenance. It was
by a strong effort he repressed the expression
of feelings which were wringing his heart,
for it was one of the tenderest that ever beat
in a man's breast.

Simonette looked at him fixedly for a
moment, then tried to undo the fastenings of
her dress. She was too weak, and made a
sign to Madame de Moldau to do it for her.
Then she drew from her bosom a newspaper
and a letter. The former was a number of
the 'Gazette de France,' and an article in it
was marked with black ink. She put her
finger upon it, and beckoned d'Auban to
come nearer. 'It was for this I went,' she
murmured. 'That is why I wanted her to
stay.'

D'Auban took the paper, and moved away
a little. She watched him with an eagerness which brought a faint colour into her
cheek. He, on the contrary, turned as white
as a sheet, as his eyes glanced over the
passage in the Gazette and then at the letter
she had brought. He came round to the
side of the bed, and whispered to Madame

de Moldau, 'Will you give up your seat to me for a moment?' She looked surprised, but immediately rose, and went out of the hut with Thérèse.

D'Auban handed the newspaper and the letter to Father Maret, and then bending down his head and taking Simonette's cold hand in his—'My poor child,' he said, with a faltering voice, 'you have killed yourself, I fear!'

'But you will be happy,' she answered, and a large tear rolled down her cheek.

'No! No! I shall always reproach myself —always feel as if I had caused your death.'

'But you must not do so, because I am very glad to die, and always wished to die for you;' and turning to the priest, she said, 'Father! did not our Lord say that no greater love could a man have than to lay down his life for a friend?'

'God may hear our prayers; you may yet live,' d'Auban cried.

'Do not agitate her,' Father Maret said; 'let her tell you quietly what she wishes, and then leave her to turn all her thoughts to the next world.'

The dying girl raised herself up a little, and uttered at different intervals the following sentences :—'I had resolved to denounce her, because I thought she was wicked, and I was afraid you would marry her . . . But I heard her tell you her story . . . and I saw how much you loved her . . . and that she loved you. Hans had told me the night before that he thought the great emperor's son was dead. But he was not certain of it. . . . I was going the next day . . . to New Orleans to accuse her . . . I went, but it was to find out if she might stay . . . if you could marry her . . . and be happy. . . .'

'Oh! Simonette, my dear, dear child, it breaks my heart.' . . Father Maret made an authoritative sign to him to command his feelings, and she went on in the same faltering voice :—

'I found it was true, and they gave me that newspaper, and M. Perrier wrote for me that letter, that you might be quite sure it was true.' At that moment the poor girl, with the quick perception which even then she had not lost, saw a shade of anxiety in

his face. 'He did not know why I asked for
it,' she added; 'I did not tell him anything.'
She paused, and then her mind seemed
to wander a little. She began again: 'I
went very quickly down the river, but I was
very long coming back . . . like what you
once said about sinning and repenting,
Father. . . . But I did not repent of having
gone . . . I prayed all the day . . .
prayed so hard . . . and rowed very hard.
But not so hard at last. I had nothing to
eat. . . . It was much longer than I thought
from the last settlement. I ate grapes as I
went along, but the rain had spoiled them
. . . and I went so slowly . . . so slowly at
last . . . and then when I could not row
any more, I screamed.' . . . 'Oh! that
scream,' murmured d'Auban; 'I shall remember it to my dying day!' 'I have
only one thing more to say; I had always
wished to die for you. Nothing, nothing
else. If I have loved you too much, I hope
God will forgive me.'

'He will, my child,' said the priest. 'If
now you turn to Him with all your heart;
and oh! my child, if a human being has

been so kind to you, and saved you from
so many evils, as I know you think this good
man has done ; if he, God's creature, has done
so much for you ; think of what His goodness
must be, of which all human goodness is but
a faint reflection.'

Simonette raised her eyes to heaven—her
lips silently moved—a smile of greater sweetness than any that had ever lighted up her face
before passed over it, and then she said in a
low voice : 'Father! during those long
weary days, and the dark solitary nights,
on the river, God was very good to me, and
made me love Him more than any one on
earth. I am very glad to go to Him. . . .
God of my heart, and my portion for ever!'
She pressed the crucifix to her breast, and
remained silent.

Father Maret made a sign to d'Auban
to withdraw. In a little while he called
him back, and Madame de Moldau and
Thérèse and the servants knelt with him
round the bed. The last sacraments were
administered, and they all joined in the
prayers for the dying. When Father Maret
uttered the words ' Go forth, Christian soul !'

a faint struggle was visible in the pallid face—
a faint sigh was breathed, and then the heart
that had throbbed so wildly ceased to beat.
'Requiescat in pace!' said the priest, and
d'Auban hid his face in the bed of moss, and
wept like a child by the corpse of the poor
girl who had loved him 'not wisely, but too
well.'

There was something shrinking and sensitive in Madame de Moldau's disposition,
which made her peculiarly susceptible of
painful impressions. It is a mistake to suppose that those who are harshly and unjustly
treated, always or even generally, become
callous to such treatment ; that after having
met with cruelty they are not sensible of
slight unkindnesses. This is so far from
being the case, that with regard to children
who for years have had blows and curses for
their daily portion, it is observed that tenderness and gentleness are peculiarly needed,
in order to avoid checking the gradual return
to confidence, and the expanding of affection
in their young hearts. The new joy of being
loved is easily extinguished. They are so
fearful of losing it, that a cold look or word

from one who for the first time in their lives
has fondled and caressed them, seems to
wound them quite in a different manner from
those on whom the sunshine of affection has
beamed from their earliest infancy. The
heart, when sore with a heavy affliction,
winces at every touch, and when, on the
contrary, great happiness fills it, the least
casual pleasure is sensibly felt. The slow
admittance of pleasurable feelings in the case
of those who grind amidst the stern necessi-
ties and iron facts of life, is one of the most
affecting things noticed in dealing with the
poor. It is akin to that gratitude of theirs
which Wordsworth said ' so often left him
grieving.'

Madame de Moldau had experienced a
slight feeling, not of annoyance or displeasure, but simply of depression, at the manner
in which d'Auban appeared to have lost all
thought of her during the whole time of poor
Simonette's dying hours. This was selfish,
heartless some people would say; and there
is no doubt that any engrossing affection, if
it is not carefully watched, is apt to make us
selfish and unfeeling. Conscience, reason and

prayer, banish these bad first thoughts more
or less speedily in those under the influence
of a higher principle; but the emotion which
precedes reflection often marks the danger
attending a too passionate attachment; and
when it is one which ought to be subdued
and renounced—which has not the least right
to look for a return or to expect consider-
ation—sharp is the pang caused by any symp-
toms of neglect or indifference. Madame de
Moldau did not know the bitter self-reproach
which was affecting d'Auban's heart; she did
not know that Simonette had lovingly thrown
away her life for the sake of bringing him
tidings which would change the whole aspect
of his destiny and of her own. But she saw
him hanging over her death-bed with irrepres-
sible emotion, his eyes full of tears—his soul
moved to its very depths. It did so happen,
that when he rose from the side of the dead,
he had abruptly left the hut, as if unable to
command himself. He did feel at that moment
as if he could not look at her. The new hope
which had come to him was so mingled with
thoughts of the closing scene, and of the sacrifice of Simonette's young life, that it seemed

unnatural—almost painful—to dwell upon it, and so he passed by her without speaking to her, and went straight into the church.

Meanwhile she suffered intensely. True, she had made up her mind to separate from him, to accept a lonely existence in a distant country, even perhaps never to set eyes upon him again ; but to think he had not really cared for her—cared perhaps for another person under her roof—the thought stabbed her to the heart, even as if no unreal weapon had inflicted the wound. Her brow flushed with a woman's resentment. The pride of a royal line—the German ancestral pride latent within her, burst forth in that hour with a vehemence which took her by surprise. Had Charlotte of Brunswick, the wife of the Czarovitch, the daughter of princes, the sister of queens and kings, been made the object of a momentary caprice? Had she tacitly owned affection for a man who had loved a base-born Quadroon? The fear was maddening ?

Yes! madness lies that way. An injury received—a wrong suffered at the hands of one loved and trusted, may well unsettle

reason on its throne—the mere suspicion of
it makes strange havoc in the brain, when we
rest on the wretched pinnacle we raise for
ourselves—the false Gods of our worship.
There is but one remedy for that parching
fever of the soul. To bow down lower than
men would thrust us. To fall down at His
feet who knelt at the feet of Peter and even
of Judas—who would have knelt at our feet
had we been there. This is the thought that
leaves no room for pride, scarcely for indignation, as far as we are ourselves concerned. It
had been often set before Madame de Moldau,
and its remembrance soon caused a reaction
in her feelings. What was she, poor worm
of earth, that she should resent neglect?
What had she done to deserve affection?
How should she dare to suspect the sincerity
of so true a heart—so noble a character?
And if, as she had sometimes thought, that
poor girl loved him, had she not a better
right to do so than herself, a wedded wife,
who ought never to have admitted this affection into her heart? And did not her untimely death claim from him a more than
common pity? The cold dull hardness in

c 2

her bosom gave way to tenderness. The sweetness of humiliation, the joy of the true penitent, took its place. She went into the chamber of death, and remained there till Father Maret came to request her to follow him to his house.

D'Auban was there. He went up to her as she entered, and seemed about to speak, but, as if unable to do so, he whispered to the Father : 'I cannot break it to her; tell her yourself.' Then, holding her hand in both his, he said, with much feeling—'Princess! thus much let me say before I go; whatever may be your wishes or your commands, my time, my actions, and my life, are at your disposal.'

She looked up in astonishment, and when he had left the room turned to Father Maret, and asked, 'What does he mean? What has happened?'

'He alludes, Princess, to a great event, the news of which has just reached us; one that touches you nearly.' He paused a minute, and then quietly added, 'The Czarovitch is dead.' She did not start, or faint, or weep. For several minutes she sate still, not knowing what was the kind of feeling which tightened her heart, oppressed her brain, and kept her silent and motionless as a statue.

'Dead!' she slowly repeated. 'How did he die?'

'It is a mournful story,' the Father answered. 'The Prince came back to Russia, as you know, on a promise of pardon; but fresh accusations were brought against him since his return. He was tried, and found guilty.'

'Oh! do not tell me that his father put him to death.'

'The account given in this paper from Russian sources is, that his sentence was read to him, and that the shock proved fatal to a constitution weakened by excesses. It says he fell ill, and never rallied again. It also mentions that he received the last sacraments before the whole court; that he requested to see his father before his death, and that they embraced with many tears. The French editor, however, throws great doubts on the correctness of this statement, and hints at the prince having been poisoned by his father.'

'Oh! surely this must be false. I cannot, cannot believe it. . . . Is it not too horrible to be true? And yet, after what I have seen. . . . Oh! why did I ever belong to them? Why was my fate cast with theirs?'

'You are not obliged; you had better not, Princess, form a judgment on these conflicting statements. Leave the doubtful, the dreadful past in God's hands. Think of it only when you pray, that your husband's soul may find mercy, and that this terrible event may have changed his father's heart.'

'He may have repented, poor Prince! He had some kind of faith, and he loved his mother. If he had had a wife who had prayed for him then. . . . Oh! my God, forgive me.' She sank down on her knees— then suddenly lifting up her head, she asked, 'How did this news come? Is it certainly true?'

'Perfectly certain—the poor girl who brought the newspaper from New Orleans also brought a letter from M. Perrier to M. d'Auban, which places the matter beyond all doubt. Will you read it, Princess?'

'Read it to me,' she answered, her eyes

filling with tears. 'I cannot see.' Father
Maret read as follows : —

'MY DEAR M. D'AUBAN,—

'A young woman, who says she is your
servant, has made a very earnest request
that I should state to you in writing that
the news contained in the last number of the
" Gazette de France," relative to the death of
the Czarovitch of Russia, is perfectly authentic.
It is most undoubtedly so; notice of this
Prince's demise has been received at the
Court of France, and their Majesties have
gone into mourning. I do not know on
what account, nor would your servant tell
me why, this intelligence is important to
you. I conjecture that it may have some
connection with a robbery of jewels belonging to the late Prince's wife, which are said
to have been sold in the colony. If any information on that subject should come to
your notice, I should feel obliged to you to
let me know of it. But I am inclined to
believe it an idle story. Wishing you every
happiness, I remain, my dear M. d'Auban,

'Your attached and obedient servant,
'PERRIER.'

'Poor Simonette!' exclaimed Madame de Moldau. 'These are then the papers she gave M. d'Auban. This was what she was pointing to when she touched her breast, whilst lying half unconscious on my knees. But what, reverend father, do you suppose was exactly her object?'

Madame de Moldau blushed deeply as she put this question, and as Father Maret hesitated a little before answering it, she said: 'Had she, as M. d'Auban thought, overheard our conversation on the night before she went away? Do you think she knew who I am?'

'No doubt that she did, Princess. She told us that she had intended to go to New Orleans to accuse you of possessing stolen jewels, but that having discovered who you are, she went, but with a different purpose. She wished to find out if you were free, thinking, I suppose, that this knowledge might greatly influence yours and M. d'Auban's fate.'

'Poor girl, poor Simonette, it was for his sake, then; but I do not see, I do not know, that it can make any difference. I

thought she had left me in anger. Thank
God, I did not resent it; but how little did I
think . . . . Good heavens, if it was for him,
Father; for his sake, she did this; what a
wonderful instance of devoted disinterested
affection! How mean, how selfish my own
feelings seem to me, when I think of her.
Even now I cannot help thinking of myself,
of the change in my fate, what it might lead
to, what it might involve . . . . There are so
many obstacles besides the one now so suddenly, so terribly removed. . . . Poor girl, it
would be sad if she had sacrificed herself in
vain. My mind is so confused, I scarcely
know what I think or say.'

'And you should not try to think, or to
resolve, whilst you are so much agitated.
The Bible says, "Do not make haste in time
of clouds."'

'But I do not feel as if I should ever be
calm again, and I hate myself for thinking
of anything to-day but the death of that
poor prince—he hated me, but he was the
father of my child. My child! my poor forsaken child. I should never have left him.
I did not know what I was doing. O!

reverend father, was it not unnatural, horrible, in a mother to leave her child? . . . .'

'You were, in a certain sense, compelled to do so, princess. Your life was threatened, and it is very probable that by your flight you saved your husband from the commission of a crime.'

'True; God bless you for those words—for reminding me of that.' She was silent for a moment, and then said, in an excited manner: 'I cannot see or speak to M. d'Auban for some days. I must be alone. I want to see no one but you and Thérèse. I don't want to go back to St. Agathe just now.'

'You would, I think, find it a comfort to remain here with Thérèse, and near the church. M. d'Auban intends, immediately after the funeral, to go and meet Simon, who must be by this time on his way back from the Arkansas. He wishes to tell him himself of his daughter's death.'

'Simonette dead!' murmured Madame de Moldau; 'dead! a creature so full of life and spirits—lying dead in that next hut! all over for her, save the great realities of another world. She ought not to have died in vain. How passionately she must have wished him to be happy! but perhaps I ought still to go.'

'Princess, that is a question you cannot decide in a moment. Time and prayer must help you to it.'

'And you, too, will help me?'

'Certainly, as far as I can. I will beg of our Lord to give you grace to resolve aright. I feel very much for you, my child.' These words were said most kindly, and went to the poor lonely woman's heart, who, at this turning-point in her life, had not a friend or a relative to take counsel with, and who dreaded perplexity beyond all other trials. There are natures to whom it is the only intolerable suffering; that have a strong passive power of endurance under inevitable evils, but to whom the responsibility of a decision is perfect anguish. In struggles between duty and inclination, between conscience and temptation, the lines are clearly defined, and each successive effort is a pledge of victory. It is like scaling a steep ascent in the free air and broad sunshine. But where conflicting duties, as well as conflicting feelings, are in

question, and the mind cannot resolve between them, the depressing effect on the
mind is akin to that of walking in a thick fog
at night amidst precipices.   Under such circumstances, a child's impulse would be to sit
down and cry.   There was something childlike in Madame de Moldau's character, in
spite of its latent energy.   It did her good to
be pitied.   Father Maret's sympathy seemed
to loosen the tight cord which bound her
heart, and she sat down in Thérèse's little
garden, and after a good fit of weeping, felt
comforted and relieved.

Over and over again she read and mused
over the details of the Czarovitch's death,
which the French Gazette contained.   A
deep compassion filled her soul for the unhappy man who had been her husband.
Womanlike, she resented his wrongs, and
shed tears over his fate.   Whilst reading the
eloquent words with which the bishops of
the Greek church had sought to obtain mercy
from him at his father's hands, she felt it had
been wrong to despise them as she had done
in former days, and that the Christian faith,
however obscured, and a Christian church,

however fallen, can speak in nobler accents and find words of greater power than cold unbelief can ever utter. Her heart softened towards those Greek priests she had once hated, and she said, 'God bless them for this thing which they have done.'

In one part of Thérèse's cabin that night was reposing the lifeless form of the girl who had just died, and divided from it only by a thin partition rested the woman in whose fate so great a change had taken place. On each pale face the moon was shedding its light. Cold and motionless was the bosom of the first, whilst that of the other was heaving like a child's that has cried itself to sleep. For the girl of seventeen all was over on earth. For the widowed wife life was opening new vistas; dream after dream filled her brain with visions of grief and joy, in wild confusion blent. Words akin to those dreams fell from her lips—

> And as the swift thoughts crossed her soul.
> Like visions in a cloud,
> In the still chamber of the dead
> The dreamer spake aloud.

Thérèse did not sleep. She was accustomed

to long night watches, and she knelt and
prayed between the two sleepers. She did
not know the secrets of those two destinies,
but she said the 'De profundis' for the one,
the 'Memorare' for the other. 'May she
rest in peace,' for the dead; 'May she live for
God,' for the living.

When the morning dawned, and the
rays of the rising sun began to light up the
silent hut, she laid down by Madame de
Moldau, and took a few moments' repose.
Once she was roused by hearing her murmur some words of the Bible; they were
these: 'Am I not better to thee than ten.
sons?'

D'Auban had attended the service for poor
Simonette's burial. He had stood on one
side of the grave and Madame de Moldau on
the other. Their eyes had not met whilst
the solemn rites were performed. It was
only when the crowd had dispersed—for set-
tlers and natives had attended in great numbers the funeral of Simon's daughter—that he
came up to her where she was still standing,
in the cemetery, and placed a letter in her
hands. She took it in silence, and held out
her hand to him. He kissed it, and with-

drew to prepare for his departure. His letter
was as follows :—

' MADAME,

'I have a few words to say, which I feel
it easier to write than to speak. Your fate
is changed, and so are my duties towards you.
From the moment I became acquainted with
your name and rank, that I knew you to be
a princess and a wife, I felt the deepest regret
that by my rashness and presumption I had
put it out of my power to devote to you as
a servant a life which I would fain have spent
in your service. That I had made it impossible for you to accept of the services which,
under other circumstances, I might have been
permitted to render to one so infinitely above
me in rank, as well as in merit. Whilst you
were forced to hide your name, whilst the
unhappy prince, your husband, was alive, I
felt constrained to see you depart from hence
alone and unprotected, and dared not even
offer to accompany you to the place you had
fixed upon for your future residence. I will
not dwell upon what I suffered ; it was one
of those efforts at passive endurance more
trying than the most painful exertions.

'Now, as I said before, a great change has taken place in your position, and I venture to lay at your feet whatever God has given me of strength and energy, to be spent, and if it please Him, consumed in helping you to reassume the position which belongs to your Imperial Highness, both by birth and marriage, and replacing you on the steps of the throne which your son is one day to occupy. I have no ties or duties which bind me in an absolute manner to any spot on earth. If you will deign, Princess, to accept me as your servant; if you will allow me to act by you as our poor friend would have done had he yet been alive, I will accompany you to Europe, and only leave you the day when, amidst your relatives, and the friends of your youth, you will stand once more acknowledged by them all as their lost princess.

'I implore you to trust me. I dare not promise to forget the past, but I can and do promise that no word shall ever pass my lips unbecoming a servant. I would not ask to live near you at Court, and be your servant there; but whilst trials and difficulties beset you, whilst you are friendless and alone,

grant me this favour. Let me be your servant. I feel nearly as old as poor M. de
Chambelle. The last few months have seemed
to add many years to my age. Let me be
your guardian. I could not brook a refusal.
It would wound me to the heart. I know
there will be many difficulties to overcome,
and a long time may elapse before your
identity is acknowledged, but that it will be
so at last I feel no doubt of; and if it is
granted to me to see you happy—I was going
to say I could be happy to part with you for
ever, but I cannot, dare not, write such an
untruth. I do not want to be happy myself;
I want to see you happy. That I can and
do say from the depths of my heart. Forgive me, Princess, if this letter ends in a less
formal manner than it began. It need not
make you distrust the promise I have made.
I have not courage to write it over again, so
I send it just as it is, with the most fervent
blessings and prayers that you may indeed
be happy, and that I may help you to be so.

'Your Imperial Highness's

'Devoted servant,

'HENRI D'AUBAN.'

This letter had been written the night before it was given to Madame de Moldau. Perhaps the tone of it might have been a little different had it been composed after the brief meeting in the cemetery; for as he looked at her, as he kissed her hand, as he felt its silent pressure, hope, in spite of himself, sprung up in his heart and made it bound. Princess as she was, the woman he loved was now free. Men's customs, their habits, perhaps their laws, stood between him and her, but not God's laws, not His commandments. The words she had once said came back to his mind: ' It is the wedded wife, not the Imperial Highness, who rejected your love.' And as he gazed at the solitary beautiful landscape, at the boundless plain and far-stretching forests on every side, he thought how insignificant were the thoughts of men in that solitude, how impotent their judgments. If she should choose to abandon altogether the old world and accept a new destiny in the land where their lot was now cast, might they not now, with safe consciences and pure hearts, be all in all to each other! But he had resolution enough

to give her the letter he had written under
a stern sense of duty, and not to add a word
to diminish its effect. He went on his way
through the forests and the deserts, and en-
countered the usual difficulties belonging to
such journeys. But bodily exercise relieves
activity of mind, and he was glad to have
something to direct his thoughts from their
too absorbing pre-occupation. Six days
after his departure he met Simon, and went
through the painful task of breaking to him
his daughter's death. The bargeman was
much afflicted by this sudden blow, but he
did not care quite so much for his child since
she had ceased to be his companion and
plaything. D'Auban gave him a sum of
money in recompense for Simonette's services
to Madame de Moldau, thinking at the same
time how little money could repay what the
poor girl had done for them. Simon was
not indeed consoled, but somewhat cheered,
by the sight of the gold; for the ruling passion is strong in grief as well as in death.
Then d'Auban retraced his steps, and stopped
that night at the little Mission of St. Louis.
He reached it just as the evening service was

going on. The scene was precisely similar
to the one so beautifully described in Longfellow's poem :—

Behind a spur of the mountains,
Just as the sun went down, was heard a murmur of voices,
And in a meadow green and broad, by the bank of a river,
Rose the tents of the Christians—the tents of the Jesuits'
mission.
Under a towering oak, that stood in the midst of the village,
Knelt the Black Robe chief with his children ; a crucifix, fastened
High on the trunk of the tree, and overshadowed by grape vines,
Looked with its agonised face on the multitude kneeling be-
neath it.
This was their rural chapel—aloft, through the intricate arches
Of its aërial roof, arose the chant of their vespers,
Mingling its notes with the soft susurrus and sighs of its
branches.

The traveller knelt down and joined in the
devotions of the Indian congregation, and
after they were ended introduced himself to
the priest, who invited him to spend the
night in his hut. The pleasure of seeing a
Frenchman, and conversing in his native language—a rare one in that locality, beamed
in the face of the good father. 'I have
been very fortunate this week,' he said ; 'for
several months past I had had no visitors,
but on Tuesday quite a large party of travellers, including two European ladies, halted
here on their way to Montreal. We had

some difficulty in putting them all up for the
night. I managed to accommodate the two
priests and one of the gentlemen, the others
slept in the schoolmaster's hut, and the two
ladies in the schoolroom. It was luckily
fine weather, and they were not very uncom-
fortable, and I had not had such a treat
for a long time. Three masses were said
the next morning in our poor little chapel.
It was the first time such a thing had happened. And they were all such kind and
pleasant people.'

Little did the good father guess, as he
good-humouredly talked on in this manner,
what anguish he was causing his guest, who,
in a voice which any one who had known
him would have thought strangely altered,
enquired the names of these travellers.

'Father Poisson and Father Roussel, and
M. and Madame Latour, and M. Maçon. I
did not catch the name of the other lady.'

'Was she tall and fair?'

'Yes, I should say so—tall, certainly.'

'Young and pale?'

'Rather pale, I think; but about ladies'
ages I never know—yes, I suppose she was

quite young. Are you acquainted with them, my dear sir?'

'I know some of them by name,' d'Auban answered, pushing away the dish which had been set before him; he could not have swallowed a morsel. There are circumstances which heighten singularly the acuteness of certain trials. He knew that he might still have to part from Madame de Moldan, though during the last few days hope had been gradually gaining ground in his mind; but he had never anticipated that such a separation would take place in an unexpected and abrupt manner. That she should leave St. Agathe during his absence, and that he should thus lose the opportunity of speaking a few parting words to her, was more than he could endure; it almost upset his fortitude. The Father noticed his paleness and want of appetite, and the way in which he unconsciously pressed his hand against his temples, as if to still their throbbing. 'I am sure you have a bad headache,' he kindly said; 'come out into the air and take a stroll—it is a beautiful night.'

D'Auban accepted the proposal, for the

hut was very close. The fresh air did him good. He took off his hat, to let it blow on his forehead. He tried to think that the second lady of the party might not, after all, be Madame de Moldau, though the others were the people she was to travel with; and only one lady had been mentioned by Father Maret's correspondent.

As they passed a small cluster of cabins the priest pointed to one of them, and said, 'Ah! there is the bedroom of our ladies. They had to sleep on mats with a bundle of moss for a pillow.'

The door was open. D'Auban stood on the threshold, and gazing into it, thought: 'Did she indeed sleep in this spot two days ago, worn out by fatigue and sorrow, or did she lie awake thinking of the past and of the future, without a friend near her? Or is she now glad to escape from that love I could not conceal, and which perhaps frightens her away? Perhaps she is seeking other assistance than mine to recover her position. She will not, I suppose, accept the services of one who has dared to love her. It would not have been wrong, however, to wait for

my return. . . . She might have spared
me this suffering.' Absorbed in these musings
he was forgetting his companion, and was
only roused by hearing him exclaim, 'Ah!
what have we here! See, one of those poor
ladies has dropped her neck-handkerchief.
It will be no easy matter to restore it, seeing
we have no postal service in this part of the
world!' D'Auban till that moment had had
a lingering hope that Madame de Moldau had
not after all been one of the ladies of that
party; but now he could no longer have a
doubt on the subject. The blue and black
silk handkerchief in the hands of the priest
was the very one he had often and often seen
round her neck. He mechanically stretched
out his hand for it. It was one of those
little things connected with the remembrance
of past happiness, which affect the heart so
deeply.

When the evenings grew chilly after hot
sunny days, or when in the boat or the sledge
on bright frosty nights, he used to remind
her to tie her handkerchief round her throat
—her white, slender, swan-like throat. It had
a trick of slipping off. He saw her in fancy

smiling as she was wont to do, on these occasions. So vivid was this recollection that a deep sigh burst from him.

'You are suffering very much; I am certain of it,' said his companion; 'you must let me prescribe for you; like most missionaries, I am somewhat of a physician.'

D'Auban seized his hand.

'I am not ill, my dear father, but it is true I am suffering. Pray for me, and forgive my strange and ungracious conduct.'

'Would it be a comfort to you to tell me your grief?'

'I could not speak of it without relating too long a story for me to tell or for you to hear to-night. But thus much I will say: missing those travellers who were here three days ago has been a terrible blow to me. One of them, the one to whom this handkerchief belonged, is very dear to me; and I shall probably never see her again.'

'But could you not overtake them, my dear friend? women cannot travel fast.'

'Do you know what road they were to take?'

'The usual one to Canada; but, to be sure,

in a country like this it would be ten chances
to one that you hit on the same track.'

This was obvious; and d'Auban, who for
one minute had been tempted to catch at
the suggestion, remembered that there were
other reasons against it. His absence from
the concessions even for a week had been a
risk, and a prolonged one might affect not
only his own but likewise Madame de
Moldau's interests; and she might be more
than ever in want of means, if she intended
to return to Europe. It might also have
been her wish by this sudden departure to
avoid the pain or the embarrassment of a
parting interview.

Observing his agitation, the priest said, in
a grave and compassionate manner, ' Perhaps
you ought not to follow her?'

' No, father ; it would not be wrong, but it
would be madness. I must, on the contrary,
return as speedily as possible to my habitation. If you have anything to write to
Father Maret I will take charge of it.'

' You know him, then?' said the priest, with
a look of pleasure.

' He is my most intimate friend.'

'Ah! well, God bless you. It is a good thing in sorrow to have a friend, and a friend like him. I will spend the night in writing, and then you can use my bed; that will suit us both.'

D'Auban remonstrated against this arrangement, but the good missionary insisted on carrying it out. He took a few hours' broken and restless sleep on the poor couch, whilst his host sat writing on an old trunk, which served at once as a chest and a table.

The first sight of St. Agathe was almost more than d'Auban could bear. He had, during his homeward journey, schooled himself to endure with fortitude his return to the place which had been her abode, and in which every object was so intimately connected with her presence, that he could hardly picture it to himself without her. But when, as he came out from the forest into the glade, it rose before him in all its cheerful beauty, so striking amidst the grand and gloomy scenery around it, his courage almost failed. But he determined to master the pain and to look that suffering in the face. Riding up to the door he gazed

on the park, the verandah, the window of
her room, and then breathing a deep sigh,
turned away, saying to himself, 'The worst is
over now,' and rode on to his own house.
When he entered, he was looking so worn
and ill, that his servant Antoine was quite
frightened. He brought him some wine, and
anxiously asked him if he had not met with
some accident. He said no; and asked if
any letter had arrived during his absence.

'No, not one, sir,' Antoine answered.

D'Auban thought Madame de Moldau
would at least have written to him. A
feeling of resentment rose in his breast, which
made him better able to conceal his feelings.
He would not for the world have uttered her
name, though he would have wished to
know the exact day on which she had left.
Wounded pride is a powerful stimulant; it
gives a false kind of strength even whilst it
embitters a wound.

He sent for his overseer and looked over
his accounts. Both the overseer and Antoine
observed the burning heat of his hands, and
that he often shivered that evening. His
face was alternately pale and flushed. They

felt anxious about him, and well they might;
for he had caught the fever of the country
whilst taking a few hours' rest in a hut by
the river-side on the last day of his journey.
The sufferings he had gone through had pre-
disposed him to it. In a few hours he was
so ill that Father Maret was sent for. For
two or three days he was alarmingly ill; and
it was evident that he was suffering in mind
as well as in body. There was in his character—and it was perhaps the only fault that
others noticed in him—a rigidity which made
him take extreme resolutions, and act up to
them with a firmness bordering on obstinacy.
From the moment he found that Madame de
Moldau had left St. Agathe he determined to
suppress in himself, by a strong effort of the
will, all feelings more tender or affectionate
than those which it was befitting for him to
entertain towards a person in her position.
He would work for her and watch over her
interests more closely than ever. If she should
ever call him to her assistance he would
obey her summons and never utter a word of
complaint; but, except when business made
it necessary, he would never pronounce her

name or allude to their former intimacy.
And accordingly when Father Maret visited
him on his sick bed he did not allude to her
departure, and abruptly changed the subject
whenever he seemed about to speak of her.
At the end of the fourth day the fever
abated, but it promised to take an intermit-
tent form, and in the intervals his weakness
was great.

Antoine watched him most carefully, and
when Thérèse offered to come and nurse him,
he somewhat scornfully rejected her proposal.
'These women,' he said one evening to his
master, ' are always fancying that nobody can
take care of sick people but themselves.
And they are often dreadfully in the way.
Ministering angels I have heard them called ;
very troublesome angels they sometimes are.
The second evening after Monsieur came
home, and when he was so ill, and I wanted
to keep the house quiet, there was Madame
de Moldau coming at the door and wanting
every minute to know. . . .'

D'Auban started up, the blood rushing
violently in his face.

'What did you say ?' he asked in a voice,

the agitation of which made it sound fierce. 'Has not Madame de Moldau left St. Agathe?'

'Oh dear, no! She was here this morning to hear how Monsieur was, and if we wanted anything. I did not mean to speak unkindly of her, poor lady! She did not make much disturbance after all, and took off her shoes not to make a noise on the boards.'

A joy too great, too deep for words, filled the heart which had so much suffered. It was visible on the face, audible in the voice of the sick man. Antoine noticed the change. He had some vague idea of what was going on in his master's mind. Perhaps his mention of the Lady of St. Agathe had not been quite accidental. He went on brushing a coat with his face averted from him.

'I should not be surprised,' he said, 'if she were to be here again this afternoon. I told her we had no more lemons, and she said she would bring or send some. As Monsieur is up to-day, perhaps he would like to see Madame, if she comes herself with them?'

'Of course, if . . . if she should wish. . .

But I ought to go myself to St. Agathe.
I think I could.'

'You! oh, that's a good joke! Father
Maret charged me not to let you stir out of
the house to-day. To-morrow, perhaps, you
may take a little walk.'

From the window near which he was
sitting, in less than an hour, d'Auban saw
Madame de Moldan crossing the glade, and
approaching his house. It was a moment of
unspeakable happiness. She was still all she
had ever been to him. She had not spurned
his offers, or sought other protection than
his. This was enough. He did not at that
moment care for anything else. Their eyes
met as she passed under the window, and in
another moment she was in the room.

'Sit down, dear Monsieur d'Auban,' were
her first words, as he rose to greet her. 'Sit
down, or I shall go away.'

'No! don't go away,' he said, sinking
back into the arm-chair, for he had not
strength enough to stand. 'For some days
I thought you were gone—gone for ever!'

'Did you? O why?'

He drew her silk handkerchief from his

bosom. 'I found this in a hut a hundred miles off, where the people you were to have travelled with slept a few nights ago. And there was a lady with them besides Madame Latour. . . .'

'O, Monsieur d'Auban, how grieved I am about that handkerchief. It must, indeed, have misled you. What a strange coincidence that you should have found it! I gave it to Mademoiselle La Marche; she was the second lady of the party. They all stopped here for a day. Had it been a fortnight ago I should now have been with them.'

'What made me so miserable was the thought that you did not trust me. That you rejected my offer of accompanying you to Europe.'

'I am not going back to Europe,' she said in a low voice.

'But, ought you not?' he answered, trying to speak calmly. 'Ought you not to resume your rank and your position—to return to your son? Is it, not, perhaps your duty to do so?' he asked, with a beating heart.

'As to rank and position, to forego them

for ever would be my greatest desire. But it would no doubt be my duty to return to my poor child, if I could do so — even at the cost of the greatest misery to myself — even though convinced that the same heartless etiquette which separated me from him as an infant would still keep us apart if I went back. It would certainly have been right to make the attempt, and if spurned and re-jected by my own kindred. . . .' She stopped and held out her hand to him. ' You would not have forsaken me.'

' Never ! as long as I live. If you were on a throne you would never see me, but you would know there was a faithful heart near you and if driven from it, O how gladly would it welcome you !'

' I know it — I never doubted it — and if it had been possible, under your protection, I would have tried to make my way to Russia, and to take my place again near my son. But I forget if I told you that, before I left St. Petersburgh, the Comtesse de Konigsmark made me solemnly promise that, as long as the Czar lived, I should not reveal to any one the secret of my existence. She knew that the emperor, even if he chose to acknowledge and receive me, which is doubtful, would never forgive those who had deceived him, even though it was to save my life. My attendants especially would be liable to his vengeance. She had interests I know which made her very fearful of incurring his displeasure. It would not, at all events, be possible for me to act in this matter without her knowledge and approval. I have written to her, and must be guided by her answer. I may hear from her any day. I cannot but think she will write to me at such a decisive moment.'

'And, in the meantime, you will stay here?'

'Yes. In any case till I get her letter.'

'And if you decide not to return to Europe, what will you do?'

She coloured deeply. 'Had we not better put off speaking of that till I see my way clearly before me? I need not tell you....'

'Yes,' he exclaimed, 'I need that you should tell me, I need to know that, if we part...'

'If we part, M. d'Auban, I shall be making the greatest sacrifice a woman can make to

duty and to her child.' This was said with
an emotion which could leave no doubt in
his mind as to the nature and strength of her
feelings towards him. From that moment
perfect confidence was established between
them. Each tried to keep up the other's
courage. Both looked with anxiety for
the arrival of the expected letters. One
packet arrived, but it had been delayed on
its way, and contained nothing of particular
interest. At last, one afternoon, as they were
busy planting some creepers round the stump
of an old tree, each thinking, without saying
it, that they might not stay to see them grow,
a boatman came up to the house, and de-
livered a letter into Madame de Moldau's
hand. She sat down and broke the seals
and untied the strings with a nervous trepi-
dation which made her long about it. He
continued to prune the newly-planted shoots
in an unsparing manner. He did not venture
to watch her face, but the sound of a sob
made him turn round. She was crying very
bitterly.

'We are to part,' he thought.

'What is it, princess?' he said; 'anything
is better than suspense.'

'My poor child! my boy!' she exclaimed.

'What—what has happened to him?'

'He is set aside; thrust out of the succession. The Empress Catherine's son named heir to the crown. Poor fatherless forsaken child! forsaken on the steps of a throne, like a beggar's infant on a doorway! O why, why did I leave him! my little Peter—my son.'

D'Auban, though he could not forget his own interest in the contents of the letter, checked his anxiety, and only expressed sympathy in her sorrow.

In a moment she took up the letter again, and said: 'I am ashamed of caring so much for my son's exclusion from the throne. Have I not often and often wished he had not been born to reign? Would not I give the world to withdraw him from the court? Would that they would let me have him! Who cares for him now? Perhaps I might go one day and steal him out of their hands, and carry him off to this desert, and bring him up in my own faith. But for the present the Comtesse de Konigsmark insists on the fulfilment of my

promise. This is what she says, M. d'Auban.
"Princess, if you should come forward at
this moment, and seek to establish your position as the widow of the late prince, and
the guardian of your son, you will infallibly
be treated as an impostor, and your claims set
aside. None of those who assisted in your
escape could venture to give their testimony
to the truth of your assertions. Your reap-
pearance at this time would involve your own
family in difficulties with the Czar, and would
expose those who saved you in the hour of
danger to the greatest danger themselves. It
might even be fatal to your son. As long as
there is no one to resent his wrongs or advocate
his cause, he is safe in the hands of the
emperor. The empress is very kind to him
now, but who knows what would be the consequences if she thought you were alive and in-
triguing against her own son. It grieves me
deeply to have to write it, but for the sake of
all concerned, I feel bound to claim the fulfilment of your promise, solemnly given at the
moment of your departure ; and I feel assured
that in doing so I am serving your own interests and those of your son. The day may

come when, in spite of the late decree, he
will ascend the imperial throne. Then, perhaps, you may safely return to Europe ; but
you know Russia too well not to be aware of
the dangers which threaten those nearest to
the throne, when not too helpless to be
feared." Nothing can be clearer. I am tied
hand and foot—cast off—never to see my
child again ; for who would know me
again years hence? who would believe me
then? Oh my boy, has it indeed come to
this!' These words, and the burst of grief
which accompanied them, painfully affected
d'Auban. She saw it in his face, and exclaimed : 'Do not mistake me ; you cannot
guess, you do not understand, what I feel.
It is very strange—very inconsistent.'

'God knows, princess, I do not wonder at
your grief. What can I be to you in comparison with your child? How can I claim
an equal place in your heart?'

'Equal! Oh, M. d'Auban, do not you see,
do not you understand that I love you a
thousand times better than that poor child,
and that I hate myself for it?'

He silently pressed her hand, and when

both had grown calm they parted for that day; he to attend to business, and she to walk to the village, where she had a long interview with Father Maret. He listened patiently to the outpourings of her doubts, her misgivings and self-accusations; to the inconsistencies of a loving heart and a sensitive conscience. It was a work of patience, for he perfectly well knew how it would end; and feeling certain that she would marry d'Auban at last, and not seeing anything wrong in her doing so, he gave it as his opinion that she had better not torment herself and him by prolonged hesitation, but agree to join their hearts, their hands and their plantations; and from that hour to the one in which death would part them, do as much good together as they could in the New World, or wherever else the providence of God called them.

A few weeks later, in the church of the Mission, Charlotte of Brunswick was married to Henri d'Auban. She had required from him a promise, which he willingly gave, that if the day should ever come when she could approach her child without breaking her promise, that he would not prevent, but on the contrary assist her to do so. As the husband and wife came out of the church they stopped a moment to pray at M. de Chambelle's tomb. As they were leaving it, she said, ' Monsieur d'Auban, you have kept your promise to him.'

' Ah! but what would the good old man have thought of such a mésalliance, Madame?' d'Auban answered.

' I would have told him,' she replied, smiling also, but with tears in her eyes, ' that the princess lies buried in the imperial vault at Moskow, and that she whom you have married has neither rank nor name—nothing but a woman's grateful heart.'

PART II.

CHAPTER I.

Sweet was the hermitage
Of this unploughed, untrodden shore,
Like birds, all joyous from their cage,
For man's neglect we loved it more.
And well he knew my huntsman dear
To search the game with hawk and spear,
Whilst I, his evening food to dress,
Would sing to him in happiness.

. . . .

And I, pursued by moonless skies,
The light of Connocht Moran's eyes.

Campbell.

O she walks on the verandah,
And she laughs out of the door,
And she dances like the sunshine
Across the parlour floor.
Her little feet they patter,
Like the rain upon the flowers,
And her laugh is like sweet water,
Through all the summer hours.

Negro Melody.

A FEW brief years will suffice to record the
history of Henri d'Auban and his wife, during
the eventful years which followed their marriage. Novelists are sometimes reproached

with dwelling on the melancholy side of life, of not presenting often enough to their readers pictures of happiness, such as exists in this world even in the midst of all its sin and suffering. But is it not the same with history? How seldom do its pages carry us through bright and smiling scenes? How few of them record aught else but crime or sorrow? The truth is that there is very little to relate about happy people. A joyous face tells its own story; a peaceful heart has no secrets. If everybody was good and happy, writers of fiction might lay aside their pens.

She, who though doomed to death had been so strangely fated not to die, and who had passed as it were through the grave into a new world, sometimes felt almost tempted to believe that the whole of her past life was a dream. That the deserted, hated and miserable princess of former days could be the same person who—now, with a light step and a gay heart, trod the sunny prairies of the New World and the mossy carpets of its wide forests, as if the blue sky over head was the dome of a vast temple, in which the varying seasons kept festival with incense-breathing flowers, and winds whispering songs of praise, seemed indeed incredible to herself, as it would have been to any one who had looked on this picture and on that. When once she had fully entered into the full spirit of a settler's life, its very freedom from conventional trammels was as agreeable to her as the boundless air to the bird set free, or the sight of the wide ocean to the liberated captive. She had never enjoyed till then a sense of liberty. The gentle formalities of her father's dull court had preceded the miserable slavery of her wedded life, and that had been followed again by all the sufferings of her flight, and of her arrival in America.

Now it seemed as if for the first time sunshine was flooding her soul. In the new atmosphere of faith and love which surrounded her, every faculty was developed, and every aspiration fulfilled. No human happiness is, however, perfect. There were moments when the very blessings she enjoyed called up a sharp pain. When her eyes had been fixed awhile on her husband's face, or on the various beauties of her home, she would suddenly turn them away, and appear to be gazing on some distant scene till tears gathered in them.

And when she became for the second time a mother, when her little girl was born, when she nursed her at her breast, when she carried her in her arms, when she saw her totter on the grass, and then fall with a scream of joy into her delighted father's arms, when she began to lisp a few words of prayer at her knee, and when, as time went on, she did not miss one of her smiles, one of her childish sallies, but noticed and dwelt upon and treasured them all; as she kissed her soft cheek, and twined her little arms round her neck, a feeling, made up of pity and yearning and a vague self-reproach, would for a moment wring her heart at the thought of her first-born, the lonely royal child in the cold northern palace far away. Sometimes she passionately longed for tidings of her kindred. Sudden and final as her separation had been from them, gushes of tender recollections would now and then arise in her soul, when some accidental word or sound, or the smell of a flower, or a feeling in the

air, recalled some scene of her childhood and
youth. Of her sister she chiefly thought;
who, on the same day as herself, had been
doomed to an untried destiny, and with whom
she had parted in the blissful unconscious-
ness of coming woes. Often after a day when
she had gathered about her all the little
children of the Mission, and played and
laughed with them to their hearts' content,
her pillow at night would be wet with tears.
These were the shadows that clouded over
her bright days, but bright they were withall,
bright as love could make them. With the
quiet enthusiasm of the German character
she applied herself to all the duties of her
new position, and governed her household
with the talent which Peter the Great had
discerned in his daughter-in-law. It was a
peculiar one she had to rule, but the charm
of her manner, joined to the goodness of her
heart, carried everything before it. She was
a little bit exacting; she liked to be waited
upon and followed about, and made the first
object of all her dependents, but they did
not love her the less for it. There are persons who are allowed to be tyrants by a sort

of common assent ; no one has any desire to
shake off the yoke, so sweetly and lightly
does it sit upon them ; but they must be the
elected monarchs of their subjects' hearts.
Nobody has a divine right to have their own
way.

Who would ever have guessed that
Madame d'Auban had been reared in a
palace who had seen her at work in her
kitchen or in her laundry by the river's side ?
And yet, perhaps, a keen-sighted observer
would have noticed the refinement of all
her movements—the grace of her attitudes
—and deemed her fit for a throne as she
stood amidst her dark-coloured slaves on
the green margin of the stream, spreading
the white linen on the grass, or wringing it
with her still whiter hands.

It was as pretty a picture as possible, with
its background of forest trees, and its che-
quered lights and shades.   D'Auban sometimes watched it from a distance, and reminiscences of his classical studies would recur
to him as he gazed on his fair and beautiful
wife and her dark attendants.   Thus were
Homer's princesses wont to direct the labours

of their maidens.   He did not feel as if his
bride was one whit less royally occupied than
if she had been holding a drawing-room.
What would have seemed unbefitting her
birth in such occupations if associated with
the commonplace scenes of the Old World,
seemed transformed into poetry when carried
on amidst the grand scenery of the New.
The wild-looking Indians; the negresses
with their bright-coloured head-dresses; the
pines, the palms, the brilliant sky, lent an
Oriental colouring to the whole scene.   St.
Agathe seemed made for the abode of a fairy
queen.   Nature and fancy had lavished upon
it all their gifts; and love, the most potent of
all magicians, had heightened all its charms.
D'Auban's fond dream had been to make it a
perfect home for the woman who had transformed his solitude into a paradise, and many
a princess, 'nursed in pomp and pleasure,' but
who had never reigned over a devoted heart,
might have envied the fate of the settler's
wife. She had her courtiers, too, this princess,
who, when once she had renounced her rank
and gained happiness in its stead, began,
with a truly royal instinct, to gather around

her a crowd of satellites, and was more
worshipped than any eastern or western
queen.   Her house was literally besieged
all day by these liege lords of every race
and colour.   Indians, negroes, and poor
whites were equally devoted to the lady of
St. Agathe.   They claimed her bounty and
her sympathy — her help, or, if nothing else,
her kind words. They brought offerings also,
and laid at her feet fish and game, and fruit
and flowers; she who had once, in her days
of gloom and misery, disclaimed all love for
' the sweet nurslings of the vernal skies,' now
gladdened with delight at the sight of the
prairie lily, the wild rose, or the blue
amorpha.   The homage paid her by the
childlike Indians was almost superstitious.
One of the hairs of the head once bowed
down in anguish at the feet of a princely
ruffian was treasured as a talisman.   Father
Maret said to her one day, ' I must preach,
Madame, against the Magnolian idolatry.   One
of your Indian worshippers wears a stone
fastened to his girdle.   I asked him what it
meant, and he said the wife of the French
chief, the white Magnolia, had set her foot on

it when she entered his cabin. I cannot
sanction the use of these new manitous.'

She laughed, and answered, 'It is all
poetry, reverend Father; poetry in action.
Now that I begin to understand the language
of these people, I am more and more struck
with the imaginative beauty of their ideas,
and the graceful form in which they clothe
them. I try to enter into its spirit, and to
reply to them in the same manner. The
other day I met an Indian, an old man, but
not of this tribe; he belongs, I think, to the
Dacotahs. He stopped, and said to me:
"Ah! my daughter, happy are my eyes to
see thee! My heart's right hand I give to thee.
The earth never blossomed so gaily, or the sun
shone so brightly, as on this day when I behold thee." I answered: "Stranger, your words
are very good, and I too give you my heart's
right hand; but whence do you know me?"
"The Mississippi," he said, "has whispered
to the Wabash, and the Wabash to the Ohio,
that the white flower of the Illinois loves the
race of the red men. Therefore, my daughter,
if thou wilt come to the land of the Dacotahs,
and to the hut of their Great Eagle, its doors

will open to greet thee in peace." Was not that
pretty, reverend Father, and much more flatter-
ing than the best-turned French compliment?'

'I am afraid, Madame,' said Father Maret,
'that the Indians will propose to make you a
woman-chief like the female suns of the
Natches.'

'And why not?' cried Madame d'Auban
gaily. 'We might both be suns, or Henri
might be the sun, and I the moon and revolve
around him. What do you say to this idea,
Monsieur d'Auban? Shall we be king and
queen of the Illinois?'

Her husband looked up into her face as
she bent lovingly over him, and said with a
smile, 'The hereditary instinct is still at work,
I see, Madame. How little we thought,' he
added, turning again to Father Maret, 'how
much ambition there is still in this deceitful
woman's heart! She has set up a perfect
sovereignty over the hearts of this people, and
is dreaming of fresh conquests.'

'Ah! I took you both in. Well, I own I
am ambitious, but it is a little your doing,
reverend Father. When one has once realised
that principle of yours, of working towards
an end, and doing everything with a pur-

pose, there is no knowing where it may
lead one. It is a little like the traveller's
story of the Flying Dutchman—when his leg
was wound up he could never stop again.
I want to convert thousands of souls; to
draw all the neighbouring tribes into the fold
of the Church; to have as many missions
here as in Paraguay.'

'Then, Madame, I see no hope of rest for
you on this side the grave,' answered the
Father with a smile. 'I never expected to
see you so fond of work.'

'There is no saying what indolent natures,
when once roused, will arrive at. Do not you
notice, reverend Father, great varieties of
character and habits amongst these Indian
nations?'

'Very striking ones, I should say. The
Arkansas and the Algonquins, as well as the
Illinois, have received Christianity with much
willingness, and are attached to the French.
With the Dacotahs and the Natches, though
in some respects more civilised, very little
progress has been made. The Dacotahs and
Choktaws are fierce, warlike races, and,
though they call themselves our friends, are
not quite to be trusted.'

'I often think,' d'Auban observed, 'that this colony is living on a volcano. Only think how insignificant is the number of our countrymen in comparison with the multitude of natives and of negro slaves we have imported; a mere handful, after all! Things are in a state in which an accidental spark might kindle a flame from New Orleans to the sources of the Mississippi.'

'Here at least,' said his wife, 'we can feel quite in safety; our dear Indians would never turn against us.'

'No; because they are almost all Christians,' said Father Maret. 'Every nation which belongs to the Prayer, as they call our religion, is attached to France. The tie between them and their pastors is a security against disaffection. It is extraordinary that the Government does not feel this, and that, intent as it is on rallying to itself the native Indians, it does so little to forward their conversion and to multiply missions. The fault does not rest with the Government in France; and M. Perrier would willingly assist the missionaries, but the Company is indifferent to all but material interests.'

'Why has it been so difficult,' d'Auban asked, 'to evangelise the Natches, the most civilised, perhaps, of all these nations?'

'They have a far more organised system of religion than any other tribe, and it is identified with their habits of life and form of government. When this is the case, it is always more difficult to obtain a hearing.'

'Do they not worship the sun, like the ancient Persians?'

'Yes, and their chief is called the Great Sun of the Natches. All his relatives are also suns, women as well as men. But he is himself the chief representative of the glorious luminary they adore. Their temples have some architectural pretensions, and their ceremonies are more plausible than the gross superstitions of the northern tribes. Our converts here are certainly wonderfully good. I do not suppose that you could find in any town or village of Europe, in proportion to the number of inhabitants, so many pious, practical Christians as in this Indian settlement. I regret to say that, for the first time since I came here, I shall be obliged to leave my flock for a while. I must go to

New Orleans to confer with my superiors.
The father provincial expects me this month.
I hope to bring back many treasures for our
mission; amongst them, a detachment of
Ursuline nuns. They are doing wonders in
New Orleans. What do you say to a log-
built convent, Madame? We must fix upon
a suitable position. There are several Indian
girls preparing to join them.'

'How happy Thérèse will be to see the
black-robe women she so often talks of!
But what will become of the Mission during
your absence, reverend Father, not to speak
of ourselves?'

'The hunting season is at hand, and our
people will soon disperse. Other years I
have followed them into the forests, and
assembled them on Sundays and festivals.'

'Ah! how I enjoyed that time last year,'
exclaimed Madame de Moldau. 'Those en-
campments round the huge pine-wood fires,
in the midst of such beautiful scenery;
the grand leafless oaks, the pines burdened
with snow, and the magnificent cascades;
how they filled the air with music till the
frost set in, and then how fine they were,

chained spell-bound in awful silence! I shall
never forget our Midnight Mass in the open
air. The words "Gloria in excelsis Deo, et
in terra pax hominibus bonae voluntatis!"
seemed so appropriate under that dark blue
sky, studded with myriads of stars, and
amongst our childlike people, as simple and
good as the shepherds of Bethlehem. Shall
we have no Mass at Christmas, reverend
Father? Shall we be for weeks, nay, months,
perhaps, without a priest?'

'Father Poisson, from St. Louis, has
promised to visit you during my absence.
You must both do what you can for our poor
people, especially the sick, teaching them to
supply, by fervent acts of contrition, for the
loss of the sacraments. The early Christians
for months, and even for years, had to endure
similar privations, and so have the English
Catholics in our days.'

'Seasons of famine,' answered Madame
d'Auban, 'teach us the blessings of abun-
dance. Henri, do you hear anything?' she
asked, observing that her husband bent forward, so as to catch a distant sound. 'Is
anybody coming?'

'I thought I heard the tramp of a horse's feet,' he said.

They all listened, but the distant sound, if there was one, was drowned at that moment by the shouts of a troop of children, at whose head was Wilhelmina, Monsieur and Madame d'Auban's little girl. They came sweeping round the corner, and appeared in front of the verandah, where her parents and the priest were sitting.

If her mother was the queen of all hearts in the little world of St. Agathe, Wilhelmina was the heiress apparent of that sovereignty. From the day when the Indian women gathered round her cradle, gazing on the white baby that looked like a waxen image, wondering over its beauty till they almost believed that the tiny creature had blossomed like a lily in the prairie, she had been the favourite and the darling of every man, woman, and child in the Mission. She was fair like her mother, her features as delicate, and the oval of her face as perfect ; but her eyes were of a deeper blue, and shaded by dark eyebrows and eyelashes. From her earliest infancy she had always looked older than she

was. In her firm step and determined
manner there was an amusing likeness to her
father. She evinced the most decided preference for the Indians over the Europeans and
the negroes. Even as a baby she was wont
to stretch out her little arms and call them
her dear brown-faces, and at a later age would
fall into a passion if anyone said white faces
were prettier. The loud, monotonous chant
of the women, unmelodious as it is in European ears, was pleasing to the child, who, in
her aërial cradle amidst the pine woods, had
been rocked by its wild music. Her playfellows were almost all of them Indians, and
their language was as familiar to her as
French or German.

Brought up in the Mission-school, and by
their Christian parents, these children were
good and innocent. There was only one
point on which Mina's parents dreaded the
effect of her constant association with them.
The missionaries had not yet succeeded in
eradicating from the minds of their converts
all their ancient superstitions. Sorcerers and
jugglers still exercised some influence over
the native Christians. It took a long time

to induce them to give up their manitous
and their fetishes. These were objects to
which a superstitious reverence was attached,
and to the possession of which were ascribed
many supernatural advantages—success, for
instance, in war and in the chase, and im-
munity from various dangers. A fetish was
sometimes an animal, or it might be a plant,
or a stone, or a piece of wood. Tales of
magic were current amongst the Indians, and
held in belief even by those who on principle renounced all intercourse with sorcerers
or magicians.

Madame d'Auban, whose mind had wan-
dered at random in her youth in an
imaginary world, peopled with self-created
visions, and unchecked by any definite faith,
and whose only ideas of the supernatural
had been drawn from the legendary lore
of her native country, and stories of apparitions, such as the well-accredited ones of
the white lady who visits the palaces of the
Teutonic kings when death is at hand, and
of spectral processions like Lutzoff's wild
rushing midnight hunt, could not always
repress a shudder at the mysterious tales of

the Indian wizards. But Wilhelmina, who from her earliest childhood had believed in angels and saints, and to whom the thought of the supernatural world was one of the brightest joys of life, utterly scouted whatever the Church did not teach, and set her face against all superstitious practices with the resolution which was even at that early age a feature in her character. If any of her companions happened to show her a manitou, she stamped with her tiny feet, and cried out, 'Throw it away, or Mina will not love you.' If they spoke of apparitions, wailing voices in the forest at night, eyes glaring on them in the darkness, invisible icy hands clasping theirs, she would shake her head, and say, 'Mina never hears those voices—Mina never sees those eyes—Mina never feels those hands—Mina makes the sign of the Cross, and, if there are devils near her, they go away.'

'But, little Lily of the Prairie,' they would sometimes urge, 'Redfeather has a manitou that makes him catch more game than any other hunter in the village.'

'I don't believe it,' Mina would answer;

and if they persisted it was true, she said,
'Then the devil helps Redfeather. I am
sorry for him, and the game he catches will
do him no good.' In this way she fought
her battles, always adhering to her principle,
and insisting on her conclusion, 'It is not
true, or if it is true, it is wicked:' she never
deviated from that line of argument. She
would not play with any child that had a
manitou, but if her companions were frightened at going home in the dark, or would
not cross a part of the forest supposed to be
haunted by evil spirits, she offered to accompany them, and they were never afraid when
they held her little hand, and she sang as
they walked along 'Salve Regina! Mater
misericordiæ!'

Mina was a most joyous child. Her
mother was sometimes almost alarmed at
the exuberance of her spirits, but there was
a deep vein of thoughtfulness in her character, and when she had once learnt to read
her greatest delight was to take a book out
of her father's library and carry it into the
garden, where she sat for hours under the
shade of a gum tree, poring over the Lives of

the Saints or Corneille's Tragedies. A child's book she had never seen : the few that might have existed at that time were not to be met with in the colony. One prevailing feeling seemed to grow with her growth, and to strengthen with her advancing years. This was her devoted attachment to the land of her birth and its native inhabitants. It made her angry to be called a French child. She once stained her face and hands with walnut juice to look like an Indian. All the high-flown sentiments to be found in books about patriotism she applied to her own feelings for this beloved country. Whilst learning history and geography from her father she always harped on this point, and exulted in finding on the map that the Seine and the Loire were mere streamlets in comparison with the Mississippi and the Ohio, and maintained that Indian Christians would never do such wicked things as the bad Europeans. She had been named Wilhelmina at Madame d'Auban's earnest request. Her father would have liked to call her Agathe, but yielded to her mother's wishes. 'But, my dearest wife,' he said, 'you will never let her know, I hope, that royal blood flows in her veins, and that she can claim kindred with crowned heads. Let her grow up, I beseech you, in the freedom and simplicity of the lot you have yourself chosen, and let no thoughts of worldly grandeur come between her and her peace. It might well turn a young head,' he added with a smile, ' to be told that she was the niece of the Empress of Austria, and the sister of the future Emperor of Russia.'

Madame d'Auban sighed. though she smiled at the same time. ' I promise you to be silent on that point,' she said, fondly gazing on her infant's tiny face ; 'but for my own satisfaction I like her to bear a name which reminds me of my childhood. It is, perhaps, a weakness, but, having broken every tie which bound me to my family, there is something soothing in the thought of one slight link between us still.'

And so the little Creole was named Wilhelmina, and called by her parents Mina, and by the Indians Wenonah, 'Lily of the Prairie.'

On the evening previously mentioned she had been mistress of the revels at a feast given by Thérèse to her scholars, and now, after dismissing her courtiers with parting gifts of maple-sugar and pine-jelly, she sat down on her mother's knees. Her father, noticing that she seemed rather pensive, asked her what she was thinking of. She raised her head, and said, ' I wish I had a brother ! Little Dancing-feet said to-night she would take her sweet-cake home to her brother, because he was good, and carried her over the brooks and up the hills when they went out to look for berries. Mother, would not you like to have a son?'

'Come to me, Mina,' cried her father, who saw tears in his wife's eyes. Mina went to him, but she too saw those tears, and, rushing back to her mother, she laid her head on her bosom, and whispered, ·Mother, have I got a brother in heaven?'

Madame d'Auban bent down and kissed her. 'My Mina,' she said, 'you have a brother; but you will *not* see him on earth. You must never mention his name ; but when you say your prayers you may ask God to bless him.'

'What is his name? Oh, do tell me his name!'

'You may say, "God bless my brother Peter!"'

'I shall say it very often,' cried Mina, throwing her arms round her mother's neck.

'Not out loud, my child.'

'No; like this.' She moved her lips, without making any sound. Her mother pressed a kiss upon them, and, looking at her husband, said, 'It is a comfort to have told her. I could not help it.' He nodded assent, but looked rather grave. He was sorry that the least shadow of a mystery should lie in his little daughter's mind. She had an instinctive feeling that her parents were both grieved at what had passed, and, as is the case with children on such occasions, she did not know exactly how to behave. Slipping off her mother's knees, she went round to Father Maret's side, and asked him to play at dominoes.

The tread of a horse was now distinctly heard coming up the approach, a very unusual sound, especially at that time of the year. In another moment both horse and rider

became visible, and d'Auban recognised one
of M. Perrier's messengers.

'What, Ferual!' he exclaimed, ' is it you?
Do you bring letters?'

'Yes, sir; a despatch from M. Perrier.'

'Oh, indeed!' He held out his hand for
it, and was about to break the seal, but
looking up, said, 'Mina, run and fetch somebody to hold the horse. You look very
tired, Ferual; you have ridden hard, and
we know through what sort of country.
Madame,' he said, turning to his wife, 'will
you give orders that refreshments may be
set before M. Ferual.'

The servants were all at work out of
doors, so Mina held the horse, and coaxed
him to eat some bits of cake out of her hand,
and Madame d'Auban went herself to the
kitchen to prepare food for the stranger.

D'Auban sat down at the table, and was
soon absorbed in the contents of M. Perrier's
letter. As soon as he had finished the first
sheet he handed it to Father Maret, and so
on with the others. When both had read
the whole despatch, the Father said—

' Your previsions are realised, sooner than we expected.'

' Ay,' said d'Auban, ' I had long feared something of the kind ; but how different it is only to anticipate such a calamity, or to have it actually present before one, almost at one's own doors ! '

' What will you do ? '

· I must go as soon as possible. I don't see how it can be avoided. I consider every Frenchman is bound to obey the Governor at this moment as if he was his commanding officer.'

' And your wife and child ? '

' I should like at once to take them to New Orleans, where they would be in safety, and then place myself at M. Perrier's disposal.'

' I suppose that would be best; not but that they would be safe here, I think. We could trust our Indians.'

· Oh ! for that matter, I believe every one of them would shed his blood for the mother and the child ; but my wife could not endure, I am sure, to be left behind, especially as you, too, are going away. No ;

we must set off as soon as we can, and must break it to her at once.'

'You have no fears for the journey?'

'Not any immediate fears. As I was saying an hour ago, I have long felt that we are living on a volcano. You notice the day fixed for the general insurrection is still some weeks distant—the 15th of January, according to our calendar. I suspect that up to that moment we shall find the Indians more than commonly friendly. But for the future of the colony! God help all those engaged in the struggle. I fear it will be a terrible one. Ah!' he said, leaning his head on his hands, 'our honeymoon is over! It has lasted nearly ten years. We ought not to repine. It is not often given to man to enjoy ten years of almost uninterrupted happiness. Here she comes! How will she bear to leave St. Agathe! And poor little Mina—what will she feel? Well, well, it must be gone through.'

'I will leave you,' Father Maret said, as he moved towards the door. 'You had better be alone to talk over this matter with your wife; and I have much to do at home.

But when your plans are settled, let me know, and on what day you will start.'

As he was walking away, Madame d'Auban called him back. He waved his hand with a kind smile, but went on; and her husband said :

'He is anxious to get home, dearest ; and I want to talk to you.'

'What is the matter, Henri ? What does M. Perrier say ? Oh ! I am sure there is something amiss ; I see it in your face. For God's sake, what is it ? Nothing that will separate us ? I can bear anything but that.'

'Not now, not at present, if you will come with me to New Orleans, where I must go at once. M. Perrier has received information that a general rising of the Indian tribes is to take place on the 15th of December — that they have planned a general massacre of the French. If the Governor had not received timely notice of this conspiracy, the whole colony must have perished. Now there will be time to avert the danger. He wishes me to come to him as soon as possible. He says my long intimate know-

ledge of the Indians will be of great service
at this moment, when the lives of Frenchmen and the fate of the colony hang on a
thread. Now, dearest wife, what do you
think we should do? For the present we
run no danger in remaining here. So many
of the Illinois are Christians, that there is no
danger of their rising against us.'

Madame d'Auban did not answer at once.
She walked onwards a few steps into the
garden, which had grown beautiful under
her care. She looked at the majestic river,
the pine forest, the grove of tulip-trees, and
all the familiar features of the much-loved
scene where for ten years she had been
happy ; and then, turning to her husband,
said the same words he had uttered a
moment before :

'Our long honeymoon is at an end ! '

' But our love . . . ? ' he tenderly whispered—

' Is holier, deeper, stronger than ever,'
she fervently exclaimed. ' Do not be sorry
for me, Henri ; all will be right if only you
will take us with you.'

' That is indeed what I wish ; I am not

afraid of our poor Indians. But who knows what might happen if they were attacked by more powerful neighbours.'

' And if we were ever so safe—if we could live on in peace whilst others were struggling and perishing around us, we would not accept of such peace as that, Henri. It is your duty to go. It is mine to follow you. If there is danger, let us meet it together.'

' Ah, madame! I thought such would be your wish. There is no doubt that I ought to obey M. Perrier's summons, and assist in every way I can in this emergency. I own I could not endure to leave you and our daughter behind. But I am also very reluctant to drag you back into the world you have so much reason to abhor.'

' I fear nothing but to leave you. And may I not be of use, also, in the hour of danger? You have taught me to work, my Henri: you can also show me how to suffer and to dare.'

' I have no doubt you may be of the greatest use, dearest wife. We may, indeed, be called upon to take a part in this struggle

—a terrible one, I fear—for evil passions
will be engaged on both sides.'

A shade of anxiety passed over her
face.

'At New Orleans there are so many
Europeans. Is there no danger of my being
recognized ? '

'Not much, I think, after the lapse of ten
years, and when you appear there as my
wife. But we must be cautious how we
proceed, and at first you must live in retire-
ment—at the Ursuline Convent, perhaps, if I
have to leave you for a while. I would
rather you were not identified even with
Madame de Moldan.'

'A likeness may strike people, but nothing
more, I should hope. We sometimes forget,
dearest, how incredible a true history may
be ; and every day makes me less like my
old self.'

D'Auban smiled, and thought the lapse of
time did not make her a whit less beautiful.
She was at thirty-three, though in a different
way, just as lovely as at nineteen.

'Then you will be ready to go as soon as
I can arrange about a boat and engage

rowers. The sooner we set off the better.
Father Maret will go with us, I think. How
little we thought, when he was talking just
now of his journey, that we should be his
companions! The descent of the river is of
course a far easier thing than its ascent.
Still it is tedious enough. But, please God,
we may return here in a few months. We
must look forward to that, my dearest wife.'

'I dare not think of it, Henri. For some
time past I have had a presentiment that we
were a great deal too happy here—happier
than people usually are. I felt certain
a change was at hand. For the last few
days I have had ringing in my ears some
lines a traveller carved with a penknife on
a plank in Simon's barge.'

'Oh! my superstitious darling,' exclaimed
d'Auban, fondly and reproachfully, 'will
you never give up believing in presenti-
ments? What are the lines you mean?'

> And if, midway through life, a storm should rise
> Amidst the dark'ning seas and flashing skies,
> With faith unshaken and with fearless eye,
> Thy task would be to teach me how to die.

'And you would teach me to die, Henri, as
you have taught me to live.'

'I will teach you anything you like, my
own love, but I don't see any particular prospect of death just now. And I look forward
to gathering plenty of strawberries next summer from the plants we set this morning. It
is a great blessing we have an overseer we
can trust. Jean Dubois will look after our
affairs as well as I could myself. Antoine
will come with us, I suppose. And now go
and tell Mina of the journey she is about to
take.'

'Henri,' she said, turning back again as
she was going into the house, 'do you know
what a feeling of relief it is when Providence decides a question long debated in
one's conscience? I have often thought our
life here was like paradise for you and myself,
but that a change might be good for Mina;
and then I scarcely ever hear now anything of that other poor child. There may
be duties to perform towards him yet. I had
never courage to say this; but, now God
calls us away, I feel it is right. Perhaps He
is doing for me what I had not strength to
do for myself.'

'Thank God you see it in that light,

dearest ; but you should have told me you had those scruples.'

'Oh, Henri ! It is easier to accept than to seek suffering.'

It was not quite in d'Auban's nature to feel this. Courage in endurance rather than in action is in general a woman's characteristic.

When it was known in the settlement that the inhabitants of St. Agathe were about to depart, though only for a few months, there was a general feeling of dismay. Not only the Black Robe was going, but the White Chief and his wife and child. It was a public calamity, and crowds came to St. Agathe to ascertain if it were true.

Mina assembled her friends on the lawn and made them a parting speech. She said she was going to the south, like the birds they used to watch preparing for their yearly flight, and that like them she would return when the winter had come and gone. She was sorry to go, and she carried away in her heart all her Indian brothers and sisters. She would bring them back gifts from the city of the white men : golden balls, such as Simon sometimes carried in his barge, and pictures like those in the church, only so small that they could hold them in their hands—and sweetmeats more delicious than maple-tree sugar. But she should not stay with the white people, she did not like white children—she could not help being white herself, it was not her fault: the lilies could not make themselves red like roses, if they wished it ever so much : she must be white whether she liked it or not.' Here the little orator paused, and one of the Indian children answered—

'We love your whiteness, little Lily; we should not love a red rose half so well. We should not think you so pretty if you were brown like us. But when you play with white children in the land where golden balls hang amidst shining leaves, do not love them as you love us; they will not love you as we do. You will get tired of golden balls and sweetmeats. You will long for the forests and the prairies. You will not complain, for the daughter of a chief never complains, even if the enemy tears out her heart. But you will die if you do not come back to us, and then we shall not see you till we go to the land of the hereafter.

In a very few days d'Auban's arrangements
were completed, a small amount of luggage
stowed in the barge he had engaged, and a
mattress placed at one end of it for his wife
and daughter. He took with him a fowling
piece, a pair of pistols in case of danger, and
also some provisions; for he did not wish to
stop at the Indian villages oftener than was
necessary. He hoped to kill game as he
went along, and so eke out their supplies till
they arrived at New Orleans. As to Father
Maret, his breviary was the heaviest portion
of his luggage. They started on a beautiful
October morning. St. Agathe was in its
greatest beauty. Madame d'Auban fixed her
eyes wistfully on the *pavillon* as the barge
glided away, and took leave of it in the
silence of her heart. She squeezed tightly
the little hand clasped in her own. Mina's
regrets were for the moment swallowed up
in the excitement of the journey, and when
the boat began to move she clapped her
hands with joy.

The descent of the stream, as d'Auban had
said, was far less trying than its ascent; still
it had its difficulties, its sufferings, and its

dangers. In some places it was difficult to steer the boat amidst the floating masses of rotten wood and decaying vegetation which impeded its progress. Sometimes a cloud of musquitoes darkened the air and inflicted the greatest torment on the travellers. They had to step on shore now and then to get provisions and purer water than that of the river. If they landed amidst the brushwood they were obliged to light fires for fear of serpents. The sun was very hot and the nights sometimes cold. They hurried on as much as they could, without feeling any considerable amount of anxiety; still they could not but long for the journey to end. Now and then they exchanged a few words with some of the natives on the banks of the river. They seemed in general well disposed, and nothing in their language or their looks gave the least intimation that events such as M. Perrier anticipated were really impending.

One evening the rowers had slackened their speed, they were lying on their oars and the boat gently drifting with the current, when on a promontory a little ahead of them appeared two persons, who hailed them as they approached, and made signs they wished them to stop. They turned out to be Frenchmen from the settlement of the Natches, who were on the look-out for Father Maret. They had heard that a priest was on his way to New Orleans. Father Souel had gone some weeks before to the district of the Yasous. Two or three persons had fallen ill since and were lying on their death-beds in great need of spiritual assistance. The next day happened to be a Sunday, and the French, together with a few native Christians, had commissioned these deputies to entreat the stranger priest to tarry for a few hours to say Mass for them, and to minister to the sick and dying. D'Auban did not much like the idea of this delay, but the need was so urgent that he did not feel himself justified in refusing his assent. The boat was accordingly moored to the shore and a single rower left in charge of it. The travelling party, escorted by the messengers, proceeded to the city of the Natches, where Christians from the neighbouring habitations had met and were awaiting Father Maret's arrival.

Mina was enchanted to land, after so many weary days' confinement in the boat, to run on the grass and to climb the hill which stood between the river and the beautiful plain in which the tribe of the Sun—for so the Natches called themselves—had built their city, or rather the immense village, the huts of which were scattered amidst groves of acacias and tulip-trees. In the centre of a square stood the palace of the Sun, or chief, of the nation. Opposite to it was the abode of the female Sun, mother of the heir-apparent. It was only as to size that these palaces differed from the other huts. All the houses were composed of one story. They were roofed with thatch interwoven with leaves. The halls were hung with mats of a fine texture and embroidered in various colours. The day was waning as the travellers approached the city. Torches of blazing pine-wood, fixed at certain distances, and carried about in the hands of the inhabitants, threw a red light over the scene, which heightened its picturesque effect. Mina's delight knew no bounds. It was like Fairy-land opening to her sight. New and beautiful flowers seemed to grow on every

side. and the golden fruit on the trees, mingling with white blossoms, filled her with
admiration. She saw, for the first time,
regular gardens and alleys symmetrically
planted. All the gorgeous beauty of south-
ern vegetation united to a degree of civilisa-
tion she had never before witnessed.

The party was received at the door of
Father Souel's hut by his only servant, an
old negro, who clapped his hands with joy
at the sight of a black-robe. He explained
in broken French all the chief of prayer
would have to do, and, with scarce a moment's delay, Father Maret hastened to the
huts of the sick persons he named to him.
D'Auban in the mean time went to visit some
of the neighbouring French colonists. He
found them unconscious of any approaching
danger, and did not think it prudent to com-
municate to them the intelligence he had
received from M. Perrier. Circumstances
might have changed since his letter had
been written, and, in any case, a panic
amongst the Europeans would only have
been likely to precipitate a collision with the
natives. In a very short time now, he

would be able to confer with the governor
of the colony on the necessary precautions
to be taken for the protection of the Europeans. One person mentioned that, a short
time ago, a deputation from the chief had
gone to M. Chépar, the commander of the
neighbouring fort, to remonstrate on some
harsh measures which the Natches com-
plained of. There had been a great deal of
mutual irritation at that time, which now
appeared to have subsided. Apprehensions,
however, were entertained of ill-will towards
the French on the part of the Dacotahs, a
fierce race, often at war with its neighbours,
and supposed to be hostile to the colonists.

M. des Ursins, the owner of one of the
principal concessions in this district, described
the Natches as a clever, cunning, but effe-
minate people, who would never venture on
any daring act, or do more than strive to
outwit their neighbours and cheat them in
their bargains. 'They have had, however,'
he added, laughing, 'the worst of it just
now in a transaction of this sort. Their hunters, which comprise, as you know, almost
all the men of the tribe, are preparing for

the winter season, and have been at the fort haggling with the officers about a purchase of guns and powder. In their eagerness to outbid each other they overdid their offers, and, I believe, our people made a good thing of it, and secured an immense supply of fowls, Indian corn, and provisions of all sorts.'

'How far is it from here to the fort?' asked d'Auban, who had listened thoughtfully to these details.

'About a league. The commandant will be delighted to see you, and to have an opportunity of sending a letter by safe hands to the governor.'

'Perhaps it would be as well that I should see him. Where does the père Souel say mass when he is here?'

'When the weather is fine, in the open air; or in the winter or rainy season, in a hut which is ill fitted for a chapel. There are not a great many Christians here, you know. We have no regular resident missionary, and no school. There have been fewer converts amongst the Natches than amongst any other tribe, I believe, with which Europeans

have had relations. They are more attached
to their form of worship than the other
Indians. We colonists are not an edifying
set, as you well know, so that it cannot be
said that religion flourishes here. Still, we
like to hear mass now and then. We have
not turned quite heathens. So, *au revoir*;
to-morrow in the field behind the hut, where,
I believe, you are staying.'

D'Auban walked back to the village. The
moon was shedding her pale light on the
trembling foliage of the acacias, the large
tulip leaves rustled in the night breeze, and
the magnolias emitted their incense-like
odour.

As he approached the outskirts of the city,
something white came running swiftly towards him, and, before he had had time to
recognise her, Mina threw herself into his
arms.

'Child!' he exclaimed, with the sort of
anger which anxiety gives, 'What are you
doing, here? Why have you left your
mother?'

'We both fell asleep when you went
away, but I woke up in a little while. It

was dull to lie down doing nothing when the moon was shining so brightly; I thought I would steal out quite softly, without disturbing my mother, and gather, in the field behind the house, some flowers to put on the altar to-morrow morning; I had seen some vases in Père Souel's room like those we have at home.'

' You should not have left the hut alone, Mina,' said her father, taking her by the hand.

' I have got these beautiful red flowers, papa, and I met some friends in that field.'

' Friends ! What friends ? '

' Two Indian boys, papa, with dark black eyes and long hair hanging down their backs, and bright feathers round their heads, and belts embroidered with red silk about their waists. The moment they saw me, one of them came and spoke to me, in a language a little like my own, but not quite the same. Yet I understood what he said. He asked if I was his little sister who had gone some time ago to the land of the hereafter. I shook my head, and then the other boy said : " Your sister's skin was of the colour of the leaves which fall in autumn, and her eyes like the berries we gather on the guava bushes. But this is a daughter of the white men with a neck like snow and eyes of the colour of the sky." But the other answered: "I am sure she is not a child of the white men. She is not like any child I have ever seen, and I should like to have her for my own. I think she comes from the great blue salt lake which some of our people speak of, or from some cloud in the sky."'

'What did you say to them, Mina?' asked her father, clasping her hand still tighter, with a vague sense of uneasiness.

'I told them I was an Indian child, father, and that I was born in a land a great way off, which belonged to another tribe, and that the Indians I loved were Christians. Then they told me that they were children of the sun, and one of them touched my hair, and said that a ray of sunshine had turned it into gold, and the other asked to look at my little crucifix—this one round my neck. He said something about the black-robe chief of prayer, and then spoke in a low voice to the other, who asked me my name. I said it was Wenouah, the Lily of the Prairie. They gave me these flowers, which I was not tall enough to gather myself. Will they not look beautiful on the altar, these bright red flowers ? '

D'Auban smoothed and stroked her head, and hurried towards the hut. The evening was beautiful; the scenery enchanting; the air soft and balmy; but he felt ill at ease. There seemed to him a heavy weight in the atmosphere. Perhaps it was only his fancy. Perhaps a storm was gathering. A few dark clouds were lying over the mountains to the westward. The lights from the pine-wood torches in the town were brighter than ever. Groups of Indians were scattered about amongst the trees, some playing at active games, some sitting in circles round men who were soothsaying and telling fortunes, after the manner of their tribe. From the trees hung cradles, in which infants were rocked to sleep by the evening breeze. At the fountain in the middle of the square, maidens were filling their wooden pitchers. Serene, lovely, and very picturesque was the aspect of that Indian city as

the moon rose high in the dark-blue sky,
as the light of myriads of stars shamed the
brightness of the pine-wood torches. Strange
it was that precisely at that moment a fit of
home sickness came over d'Auban such as he
had never felt in the wilder northern regions
he had so long inhabited. But in this hour
of serene beauty, in this spot of luxuriant
loveliness, he thought, with a pang that
seemed to cause him absolute physical pain,
of the smell and feeling of the briny, damp
westerly wind as it used to blow in his face
on the heights of Keir Anna ; and of the bold,
brave men who had carried him on their
shoulders in the days of his childhood. He
longed for his native land ; for a glimpse of its
cloudy sky, with a feverish longing like that
of a dying man on the battle field for a glass
of cold water. He turned away with loathing
from the sight of the fair Indian valley
studded with white huts and gleaming with
lights which glowed amidst the oleanders like
the fire-flies in the groves of Italy, and hurried
to the hut, where his wife had just started
up from the profound sleep of fatigue,
and missed Mina from her side. At that

moment Father Maret came in also. He
had been visiting the sick ever since his
arrival, and administered the last sacraments
to two or three who were dying.

'To-morrow morning,' he said, 'I shall
have to go and give Communion to an old
Christian sachem at some distance from the
village, and as soon as I return I must say
Mass in the field behind this hut. Almost
all the Christians will come. We can depart
immediately afterwards.'

'The boys who gave me the bright red
flowers will be there,' said Mina ; 'they told
me so. They said, " We will take care of you
to-morrow, little sister of the children of the
sun. We will take you to our mother." '

'What did they say?' said d'Auban,
sharply ; 'repeat their words exactly.' Mina
did so, and then said : 'Father, do let us
stay another day in this beautiful village.'

'God forbid,' murmured d'Auban. 'This
place kills me. The very smell of the flowers
seems to poison the air. I never hated any
spot so much. Now let us try to eat something, and then get to sleep.'

Soon the mother and the child were slumbering quietly side by side on a mat, with some cloaks for pillows. Father Maret took his breviary out of his pocket, and said : ' It has been a good day's work, my dear d'Auban. What a blessed thing it is to help a poor soul on its way to eternity! Thank God we stopped here. It has not been in vain. Several Christians would have died without the sacraments if His Providence had not conducted us to this place.'

' You look quite worn out,' said d'Auban. ' Surely you will not say your office now : you will take some rest ?'

' It will be time enough to rest to-morrow,' answered the priest, with the smile which his friends knew so well, and which lighted up his pale face at that moment with more than usual brightness. Long did d'Auban remember those words, and the smile which accompanied them. For some minutes he watched the priest saying his office, and then his own eyelids closed, and he fell asleep.

CHAPTER II.

Woe, woe to the sons of Gaul!
. . . . . .
They were gathered, one and all,
To the harvest of the sword,
And the morning sun, with a quiet smile,
Shone out o'er hill and glen.
. . . . . .
Aye the sunshine sweetly smiled,
　As its early glance came forth.
It had no sympathy with the wild
　And terrible things of earth.—*Whither*.

Odours of orange flowers and spice
　Reached them from time to time,
Like airs that breathe from Paradise
　Upon a world of crime.—*Longfellow*.

BEFORE the sun had risen, just as a faint ray
of light was dawning in the east, Father
Maret was on his way to the hut of the old
sachem, whom he had promised to visit that
morning. When he arrived there a noble-
looking Indian boy opened the door for him,
and pointed to the couch where the sick man
was lying. Whilst the priest was adminis-
tering the last sacraments to the sachem, he

went out of the hut, and stood there gazing, with folded arms and mournful brow, at the sky, from which the stars were gradually disappearing.

When the Father was preparing to take leave of the old man, he detained him and said, ' Good Father, call my son Ontara ; I would fain speak to him in your presence, and make him my parting gift. He is one of the sons of the Woman Chief; his father was a famous warrior who died in the war with the Choktaws. He has been as a son to me since the time I carried him in my arms, and taught him to shoot and to swim. He is good, and the Great Spirit sends him higher and better thoughts than to other youths of his age. But he believes not yet in the Christian prayer. The words I have spoken to him have fallen unheeded on his ear, like the seed scattered on the hard rock. But I will give him this crucifix, which the Black Robe of the Yasous gave me when I was a prisoner amongst that tribe, and he will keep it for the love of Outalissi, till the day when the voice of the Great Spirit speaks to his soul, and he believes the Christians' prayer.' As he said this a change came over the features of the old man, and the priest, who saw that death was at hand, hastened to summon the boy. His dark fearless eyes fixed themselves on the face of the dying sachem, who said—

'My son, take this, my greatest treasure. You will one day know its value.'

'Is it a manitou?' asked the boy.

'No, my son; it is the image of Him who died upon the cross; of the Son of the Great Spirit whom Christians adore.'

'I cannot belong to the Black-robe's prayer,' the boy said; 'I am a child of the Sun.'

The old man's eyes beamed with a sudden light. 'My beautiful one,' he cried, 'my hunter of the hills, the Great Spirit will make thee one day a fisher of men.' The energy with which these words were pronounced exhausted the speaker; he fell back in a swoon. While the missionary was striving to recall life and consciousness to the sinking frame, the boy hastily snatched the crucifix, which had fallen from his hands, and hid it in his bosom.

A few moments afterwards the aged sachem breathed his last, and whilst the priest, kneeling by the side of the corpse, repeated in a low voice the 'Miserere,' the Indian youth struck up a death-song, in which were blent, with great pathos, his own impassioned regrets, praises of the dead, and previsions as to the destiny of the departed spirit in the islands of the blessed, in the kingdom of the hereafter. The hour which had been fixed upon for Mass was arrived. Madame d'Auban and the Père Souel's negro servant had arranged the altar on the greensward behind the hut: a sort of plain which extended from the village to the forest. Mina had ornamented it with nosegays of red and white flowers, and festoons of the trailing vine. The Père Maret returned just before the appointed time. He had to hear confessions before beginning the Holy Sacrifice, and stayed in the hut for that purpose. Meanwhile the French colonists and a small number of Indian converts emerged from the shadowy depths of the neighbouring groves, and seated themselves upon the grass. Men, women, and children were there. Even the least religious amongst the emigrants felt a pleasure at the thought of hearing Mass again.

At last the Père Maret came out of the hut with his vestments on, and the people knelt down before the altar. He began by reading some prayers in French; then he preached a short sermon. D'Auban, who was to serve his Mass, was standing a little behind him. He saw that the congregation was still gradually increasing; more and more Indians were approaching from various directions; quietly, unobtrusively, they drew near. There was no sound of feet on the smooth grass. They stood in a respectful attitude, motionless like statues; rank after rank of these sable forms ranged themselves around the worshippers; not a footfall, not a whisper was heard; it was like the snowdrift which accumulates noiselessly in the silence of night; nothing was heard but the voice of the preacher. When the sermon was ended, and he had given his blessing, he turned towards the altar. D'Auban glanced at the spot where his wife and his child were kneeling, with their heads bowed down to receive that blessing, and in that one glance he took in the

aspect of the whole field; it was now crowded
with Indians; not one spot was left unoccu-
pied, not one issue open. The Père Maret
began Mass.

' Judica me, Deus, et discerne causam meam
de gente non sancta. Ab homine iniquo et
doloso erue me.' With what a strange force
and meaning those words fall on d'Auban's
ear! The alternate sentences are uttered.
The Confiteor is said, first by the priest,
and then by the server in the name of the
people. Then the priest goes up to the altar,
first to the right side to read the Introit, a
short passage from the Scriptures; then to the
centre, to cry out for mercy for himself and
others. ' Kyrie Eleyson,' he says. ' Kyrie
Eleyson!' answers the server. Ay! God
have mercy on them both ! God have mercy
on all present!

A shot is fired, and the priest falls upon
the flowery sod at the foot of the altar,
beneath the cloudless sky, in the bright sunshine, robed in his white vestments; like a
soldier on duty struck down at his post.
D'Auban's first movement is towards him.
He kneels by his prostrate form. The wound

is mortal; life ebbing fast. One last word
the dying man struggles to utter. D'Auban
puts his ear close to his lips. 'The young
Indian, Ontara,' he whispers, and then he
breathes a sigh and dies. When d'Auban
raised his head the scene before him was one
of wild and horrible confusion; the work of
slaughter had begun. A cry of despair burst
from him. Paralysed one moment by the
hopelessness of the calamity, he stood like one
transfixed, his eyes turned towards the spot
where he had last seen the treasures of his
heart; the next he made a desperate rush in
that direction, but crowds of armed Indians
encircled him on every side. The shrieks
of the murdered were in his ears. The bodies
of his dead countrymen flung at his feet.
'Kill him,' cried the Indian who seemed to
command the rest. 'Kill the companion of
the Black Robe! Destroy every Frenchman!
Slay every white man! Let not one escape to
tell the fate of the others! But do not kill the
women and children; the Great Sun of our
tribe orders that they shall be kept as slaves.'
D'Auban caught the sense of these words,
and though his brain seemed on fire, he was

in the full possession of his senses. Quick as
lightning the thought struck him, that to
surrender his life at that moment was to doom
his loved ones to hopeless misery. If God
gave him strength to make his escape, help
might yet be obtained. To save himself was
to save them. The blood rushed back to his
heart, and strength returned to his limbs.
With a wordless prayer to the God of Samson
and of Joshua, and a passionate invocation to
the Immaculate Mother, he dashed his powerful frame against his numberless foes, and
made his way through the infuriated crowd,
who shrunk back appalled by his apparently
superhuman strength. Once, when surrounded and all but overwhelmed by a rush
of assailants, a young Indian sprang upon
him, and seemed about to drag him down to
the earth; but, by a sudden movement, he
threw himself back on his advancing countrymen, checked them for an instant, and opened
for d'Auban a passage through their ranks.
During the instant he had grappled with him
he whispered in his ear, ' Do not fear
for the white woman and her child; Ontara
will protect them.' With a speed which

baffled even the swift-footed Indians, d'Auban
ran towards the river, and sprang into the
canoe of the barge with which one of his
boatmen had remained the night before.
Cutting with a knife the rope that fastened
it to the shore, both began to row for their
lives. The natives pursued them. They had
boats also. They had sworn by the great
Sun that not a white man should escape.
Arrows whizzed in the ears of the pursued,
and the savages were gaining upon them.
For one instant—it was a desperate expe-
dient—d'Auban laid down the oars, and
seized the fowling-piece lying at the bottom
of the barge. He levelled it at them. The
pursuers, terrified at the sight of the gun,
dashed aside and slackened their speed. He
loaded the piece and fired. 'It is a phantom
boat,' cried the Indians, 'no mortal man
could row so fast!' and they turned back.
After some hours, during which d'Auban had
to keep up, by promises and encouragements,
the courage of the man who shared with him
the desperate exertions of those fearful moments, he laid down his oars, and steered to
the shore.

' Is this the way to the French fort?' asked his companion, who supposed they were making for Bâton Rouge.

' No,' answered d'Auban; ' by this time the French at the fort are probably massacred. But hence we can proceed to the district of the Choktaws, a tribe which hates the Natches, and to whom the tale we have to tell will be like the sound of their own war-cry. You may follow or leave me as you please. Nay, you had better take the boat, and carry the intelligence of the massacre to the first European settlement you can reach, and tell the commander or the resident, whoever he may be, in the name of huma-nity, to concert with his neighbours imme-diate measures of relief for the captives.'

Then d'Auban plunged into the woods, and hurried on his way to a village of Choktaw Indians not far from the stream. There he made an appeal to the inhabitants, and with their own sort of wild eloquence called upon them to rise and follow him to the rescue of the wives and children of the white tribe. The flame which his words kindled spread from wigwam to wigwam, awakening the

fierce antipathies of race as well as rousing
the sympathy of men whose hearts were
stirred within them by the expressions of
anguish which broke forth from a heart torn
by conflicting emotions of hope and of terror.
The appeal of the white man was heard. The
chief of the tribe rose like a lion from his
lair; seven hundred warriors gathered round
his standard, and, with tomahawk in hand,
marched under d'Auban's guidance across the
pathless savannah and the primæval forest,
towards the sunny plain where the Natches
were triumphing over the slaughter of the
white men, and insulting the pale women and
the scared children of the murdered French.

It took days to prepare, days to effect this
march; days that were like centuries of
anguish; days during which d'Auban's hair
turned white, and lines were stamped on his
forehead which time never effaced.

When Madame d'Auban had seen the Père
Maret fall, she had risen to her feet, and
stretched her arms towards her husband,
whom she had caught sight of for an instant
supporting the form of the dying priest. But
soon she could discern nothing more amidst

the dreadful scene which ensued. She could only, in a half-kneeling, half-sitting posture, clasp her child to her breast, and listen with a cold shudder to the shrieks of the dying and the savage yells of the murderers.

In a short time she felt her arm grasped, and looking up in speechless terror at the Indian who had seized it, she heard him say, 'You are my slave, pale-faced daughter of the white man. Henceforward you shall serve as the black skins have served the children of the Sun.'

Mina, who understood the language of the natives better than her mother, pushed back the Indian with her little hands, and cried out, ' Where is Ontara, the son of the Woman Chief? Ontara!' she cried out in her child- ish, shrill, and yet sweet voice. 'Ontara! help.' The boy she thus called appeared at that moment in sight. He rushed to the spot where both mother and child were wringing their hands, and refusing to follow the Indian, whose hands were dripping with blood. He flourished his tomahawk over the head of the latter—bade him with a tor- rent of imprecations resign his captives, who

were the slaves, he said, of his mother the
Woman Chief, and making a sign to Mina,
he prepared to lead them away. The child,
less bewildered than her mother, and full of
confidence in the protection of her playmate
of the preceding day, whispered to her,
'Come, mother, come away! They will kill
us if we stay here. That dreadful man will
come back again before my father returns to
help us.'

Madame d'Auban rose, and, with eyes
glazed with despair, gazed on the frightful
scene—the lifeless corpses, the deserted altar
with its red and white flowers still unfaded,
and the blood running on all sides.

'Henri!' she cried in a loud voice,
'Henri! have they murdered you, my beloved?' Wild with grief, and dragging Mina
by the hand, she rushed to the spot where
the priest was lying dead, and falling on her
knees by the lifeless form, she clasped her
hands, and, as if he who had been as an angel
of God to her on earth could still hear her
voice, she cried out, 'O Father, dear Father!
where is he?' No audible answer came from
the icy lips. The eyes which had looked so

kindly upon her in life, did not turn towards
her now. But from that face, calm and
beautiful in the serenity of death from the
silent lips which for so many years had uttered
none but words of holiness and peace, an
answer came in that hour of distracting woe,
as if speaking from the grave or from the
skies where the pure spirit had fled. She
bowed down to the ground, e'en as by a
martyr's side, and reverently kissed the hand
which had so often blest her, and then, with
a great patience and a great strength, she
raised her eyes first to the cloudless sky, and
then once more on that scene of horror and
desolation, where neither amongst the living
or the dead could she see her husband.

'Fiat voluntas tua,' she murmured with a
sublime effort of resignation, always more
difficult during the anguish of suspense than
in the hour of hopeless certainty.

The Indian boy had followed them, and
was gazing with an unmoved countenance on
the features of the dead. 'Follow me,' he
said, pointing to the palace of his mother
the Woman Chief. When they had arrived there, he ushered the captives into her

presence. She was seated on a mat surrounded by her attendants. The young chief
said something to her, and she nodded assent.
He made a sign to Mina to approach. The
child looked up into the face that was looking
kindly upon her, and said, with a burst of
tears, 'My father! give me back my father!

The Woman Chief shook her head, and
answered, 'All the white men must die. But
the child of the white man shall live and
serve the children of the Sun!'

Mina gave a piercing cry. Ontara led her
away, and whispered in her ear, "Straight
as an arrow from a bow, and swiftly as a
feather before the wind, the White Chief
has gone down the river, far from the land
of the Natches.'

Mina ran to her mother, clasped her arms
round her neck, and said to her in a low
voice, 'My father is yet alive! He is gone
down the river. The young chief says so.'

'Then there is still hope for us,' murmured
Madame d'Auban, as she pressed her child
to her heart. 'God is merciful! That hope
makes life endurable, and for thy sake, and
perhaps for his, I must try to live, my
Mina.'

And then she, who had already gone
through so many and strange vicissitudes,
the daughter and the sister of princes, the
spoilt child of her father's little Court, the
victim of the fierce Czarowitz, the whilom
happy wife of the French colonist, began
that night her work as the slave of her
Indian captors—meekly, courageously, as
one who had been schooled in the lessons
of the Cross.

All the wives and children of the murdered Frenchmen were condemned to the
same doom, and in the anguish of bereave-
ment, some of them with nerves and feelings
almost to phrensy sore, many of them without any religious support and consolation—
for a great number of these European emigrants, through neglecting to practise their
religion, had almost lost their faith—found
themselves in presence of the greatest imagi-
nable calamity without any human prospect
of relief.

Their Indian masters exulted in their presence at the tragical fate of their victims,
and spoke openly of the massacre which
was to take place on a particular day, at
every place where there were French settle-

ments amongst all the tribes on the shores
of the Mississippi, as far as the great lakes
beyond its sources, or the sea at its mouth.
Not one Frenchman, they boasted, would
survive to carry the news to the land they
came from. The new French city, and every
fort and habitation in the country, would be
levelled to the ground, and the Indians who
had learnt the Frenchmen's prayer, and who
tried to save the life of a black robe, were to
be tied to a stake and burnt at a slow fire.

The usefulness of their new slaves induced
the savages to spare their lives, and even to
treat them with some degree of humanity.
This was at least in most instances the case.
They were delighted to make the European
women sew and make up garments for them
out of the skins of beasts and the pieces of
cloth seized at the Fort where M. Chépar and
all his companions had been murdered. The
arrival of several carts laden with goods at
that military station a day or two before had
excited the covetousness of the chiefs and
the sachems, and induced them to hurry
operations and give the signal of murder and
plunder before the day appointed for a
simultaneous rising throughout the colony.

The sight of some of these articles of European manufacture drew tears from the eyes of the poor captives, who saw in them many a remembrance of their native land. Homely bits of furniture; pieces of cloth and linen which bore the stamp of some manufacturing town which some of them had once inhabited; cups and glasses and plates such as were in common use amongst the bourgeoisie of that epoch, and many of these things were wrapt up in numbers of the 'Mercure,' or the 'Gazette de France,' or the 'Journal de Trévoux,' which were read with eagerness and wept over by the women, before whose eyes rose in those moments visions of some old picturesque French town, or of some valley in Provence or in Normandy, or of the narrow streets of Paris—a city which always preserves a powerful hold on the affections of those who have been born and bred within its precincts. Dreams of its bright river, its quaint buildings, sunny quays, and shady gardens, have haunted an exile's sleep full as often as the snowy summits of the Swiss alps or the golden groves and myrtle bowers of Italy.

Madame d'Auban and her daughter were

treated gently enough, owing to the protection of the young chief Ontara.   Their
cleverness at needle-work also obtained for
them the good graces of the woman Sun,
who was delighted to appear before her subjects decked in European finery.   Most of
their time was spent in this employment.
They sat on the grass in a grove of acacias
behind the palace hut, and worked several
hours a day.   Madame d'Auban found relief
in this manual labour to her tormenting
thoughts.   Mina helped her eagerly or
wearily, according to the mood of the moment.   Children cannot endure the ceaseless
pressure of sorrow or anxiety.   When the
uncertainty about her father's fate pressed
upon her, she hid her head in her mother's
bosom, and gave way to passionate weeping ; or when she saw that mother looking
ing pale and worn and working like a slave,
her zeal in assisting her was unbounded.
But if her friends the Indian youths appeared,
the wish to play was irresistible.

Both the young chiefs neglected other
amusements, and even the more serious
business of hunting and fishing, in order to

play with the little white maiden, who was to them a perfect vision of beauty and delight. It was a pretty sight, the fair captive child sitting under a hedge of oleanders between her two Indian playmates, who were like each other as to colouring and features, but whose countenances were strikingly dissimilar. There was something noble and refined in Ontara's person and manners—a gentleness which, in a European, would have been thought good breeding. His movements were slow and graceful, and his eyes had the pensive, almost mournful, expression peculiar to his race. Ossco's face was a cunning one, and if anything irritated him a malignant light gleamed in his deep-set eyes, which were at those moments more like those of an angry animal than of a man. He was related to the royal family, but not a son of the reigning sovereign. His wonderful quickness and agility had made him a favourite with the young chief. They were constant companions, and equally devoted to the little white captive.

One day Ontara brought her a cluster of the waxen blossoms of the Mimosa. She wove them into a wreath, and with some beautiful feathers Osseo had just given her, made a crown which she laughingly placed on her head. A sudden gloom darkened Ontara's brow, and he spoke angrily to Osseo. Angry glances and gestures followed. Mina instantly pulled to pieces both the garland and the crown, and making a nosegay of the feathers and the flowers, placed it in her breast. She had caught the habit of expressing her thoughts by signs, and was as quick as the Indians themselves in the use of symbols.

Osseo pointed to the nosegay and said, 'The flowers will be dead and drop off to-morrow, but the feathers will live in the maiden's bosom till she is as tall as her mother.'

Again a dark look gathered over Ontara's brow, but Mina hastened to reply—'The leaves may lose their colour, but they smell sweetly even when they are dry and dead. The feathers never smell at all. But they are very pretty,' she added, with such a bright smile that Osseo exclaimed—

'In your eyes, little white maiden, there

is a more powerful fetish than the one I carry in my bosom ;' and thrusting his hand in his breast, he showed the head of a serpent.

Mina shuddered, and said that a fetish was a bad thing, and that she hated serpents. There was no fetish in her eyes, she was certain, and no serpent in her breast.

On the following morning, Osseo came to the Acacia Grove, and told Mina to come with him into the woods, and that he would give her more beautiful flowers than Ontara had brought her the day before, and a bird that would imitate the sound of her voice. She looked wistfully at her mother, for she longed to run across the fields into the forest ; but Madame d'Auban shook her head, and bade her sit down to her work. She told Osseo that Mina belonged to the woman chief, and could not go out without her leave. Osseo's eyes gleamed with anger, and he threatened to drag the child away. He said she was his slave, and he would compel her to go with him. Terrified at this youth's looks and manner, Madame d'Auban resolved to place Mina under

Ontara's protection. She felt an instinctive
confidence in his generous nature, and knew
well that if an Indian once adopts anyone as
his sister or his child, he faithfully fulfils the
duties he thus assumes. So the next time
the young chief came to the palace, she made
him understand that Osseo called Mina his
slave, and threatened to carry her away.
'Will you be her brother?' she asked, with
a trembling voice. 'Will you protect her,
Ontara?' The eyes of the Indian boy
had flashed fire when he heard of Osseo's
threats; and when Mina's mother made her
appeal, he made a sign to them both to follow
him. He led the way to the assembly of the
sachem, and, in the presence of the Sun his
father, he solemnly, according to the custom
of his tribe, made her his sister; and as a
token of this adoption, he placed his hand on
her head, threatening at the same time, with
a loud voice, death to anyone who should
molest her. 'She is my sister,' he cried.
'She has returned from the land beyond the
grave. She went away when the leaves were
falling off the trees, and now she has come
back with the green leaves and the flowers,

with golden hair and sunny eyes. No one shall dare to touch her. She is a daughter of the Sun.'

Madame d'Auban looked gratefully at their young protector, and raised her hand to her lips—a token of friendship which he understood.

Mina was overjoyed. 'I have a brother now,' she cried, and threw her arms round the boy's neck. There was something entirely new to the Indian youth in the child's innocent affection, and in her way of showing it. It touched a chord in his heart which had never yet been moved. From that moment she became dearer to him than aught else on earth. Her mother's trust in him, her soft kiss, and the name of 'brother' which she gave him, made life a different thing to Ontara from what it had yet been. He had never shed a tear—his countrymen do not weep—but a strange sensation rose in his throat, and he turned away, not understanding what it could mean.

On one of the long weary days which had elapsed since that of the massacre, Madame d'Auban was sitting at her work on the grass

near their hut, and Mina by her side. A
Frenchwoman, who was carrying a pitcher on
her shoulder, stopped to speak to them on
her way to the well. She was the widow of
M. Lenoir, one of the murdered officers at
the fort, and a slave in the chief's palace.

‘Ah!’ she exclaimed, ‘Another companion in adversity! May I ask your name,
Madame?’

‘Madame d’Auban.’

‘Ah! Madame d’Auban—the wife of the
. . . Should I say the late—Colonel d’Auban?’

It is easier under certain circumstances to
bear positive unkindness than an irreverent,
well-meaning handling of a throbbing wound
in our hearts; and perhaps the greatest trial
of all is the sympathy expressed by those
who think their sorrows are like our sorrows,
when they no more resemble them than the
prick of a pin does the stab of a dagger.

‘Ah!’ sighed Madame Lenoir. ‘My poor
dear husband! He would come to this horrid
country to make his fortune, and Fortune has
played him a terrible trick! He was one
of the first killed by those demons that
dreadful morning.’

'Were you here, Madame? and was your husband also massacred?'

Madame d'Auban felt as if she was laid on the rack, 'I live in hope . . .' she murmured, but could not finish her sentence.

'My father was not killed,' said Mina. 'I am sure he will come back and take us away.'

'Ah! M. d'Auban escaped. Je vous en fais mon compliment. It was, indeed, a piece of luck. I wish my poor dear husband had been as fortunate! But he was what I call an unlucky person. If there was a possibility of getting into a scrape or a difficulty, he was always sure to do so. I used to say to him, "My friend, nothing ever succeeds with you. You were certainly born under an unlucky star. The Fates did not smile on your cradle. You never do the right thing for yourself." Ah! poor man, he used to shake his head and say, "Well, my dear, I almost think you are right. I never took an important step in life that I did not repent of it." You see he had great confidence in my judgment.'

'Was yours a happy marriage, my dear Madame? Oh! pardon me, if I distress you.

Our common sorrows—for no doubt you are
not quite easy about your excellent husband's
fate, even though you are so much less to
be pitied than I am—seem to me to establish
quite an intimacy between us.' Is this
charming young lady your only child,
Madame?'

Mina gave a quick glance at Madame
d'Auban's face. The talkative stranger had
trod unawares on the sacred ground which
her mother and herself never approached but
on their knees.

'She is my only little girl,' Madame
d'Auban nervously said, and hastened to ask
—'Have you any children, Madame Lenoir?'

'No; and indeed I am very glad of it.
M. Lenoir used to regret it; but I have said
to him, many times since we came to this
country, "Who was right on that question,
M. Lenoir? I suppose you will admit that a
wife is quite a sufficient encumbrance, as
you stand at present situated?" "Oh, quite
sufficient, my dear, quite sufficient," he would
answer. I must do him the justice to say he
did not often contradict me. If I had had any
children, I should have been dreadfully afraid

of their becoming like those young Indian devils.'

'The Indians are not all devils,' cried Mina. 'I love the Indians.'

'O fie! mademoiselle! Love those wicked Indians who murdered the good priest and my poor M. Lenoir, and all the Frenchmen! It was not their fault, I suppose, that your papa escaped?'

'It was one of them that helped him to escape, I know; and I love him and our brave Illinois, and the Choktaws, and the Dacotahs, and many others.'

'I have never heard,' cried Madame Lenoir, 'of all those savages you speak of little lady; but I know that, for my part, I should like to see every Indian burnt alive, and their horrid country swallowed up in the sea.'

'And I should like to see you in the sea, and I should not pull you out,' cried Mina, choking with passion.

'Oh, you little monster!' exclaimed Madame Lenoir.

'Mina, what are you saying?' said her mother, in a severe manner.

'But, mother, why does *she* say such wicked things? Because there are some cruel Indians, must we hate them all?'

'We must not hate even the cruel ones, but pity and pray for them.'

'Well, pious people have strange notions!' ejaculated Madame Lenoir, 'and they bring up their children very badly, I think. It is very extraordinary how unfeeling devout persons are! Ah! we cannot expect to find much sensibility in those who have not known what suffering is. Good evening, Madame d'Auban. I had hoped we might have proved a comfort to each other in our mutual sorrows, but——'

'Do not hurry away,' Madame d'Auban kindly said. 'Our trials are indeed great; and we ought to try and help each other. Do not be vexed with me.'

'Oh, for that matter, I have a very happy disposition and a particularly sociable temper. But let me advise you, as a friend, not to let that little lady get into the habit of talking too much. One never gets rid of it in after-life. And do not make a dévote of her. Too much religion is a bad thing for children.'

A faint shadow of a smile crossed Madame d'Auban's lips. Meantime Madame Lenoir was lifting up with difficulty her heavy pitcher.

'It will be heavier still when filled with water,' she said, with a deep sigh, 'and my shoulder is already aching with its weight! But I have been threatened with blows by a cross old Indian, in case I do not do her bidding.'

The poor woman sat down on the grass, weeping bitterly. It was a selfish, uninteresting grief, but pitiful to witness—like the sufferings of a fly crushed by a wheel.

'Ah! there is Ontara,' cried Mina, clapping her hands. 'Now you will see that he will help me to fill your pitcher. May I go to the well with him, mother?'

Madame d'Auban assented, for the fountain was not far off. The young chief took up the pitcher, and Mina laid her hand on the handle, to help him, as she said, to carry it. He looked at the little white hand with wonder and admiration. He did not know anything about gloves, or he might have exclaimed, like Romeo:

O that I were a glove upon that hand!

Mina talked to him eagerly as they walked along ; and he called her his ' white lily,' his ' beautiful Wenouah.'

When they had reached the fountain, and were letting down the pitcher into the water, she said :

' Oh! how I do wish . .' and there stopped short.

' What does my flower wish ? ' Ontara asked. ' Name thy wish, and I will ask my father the Sun to give thee whatsoever thou desirest.'

' I do not want anything he can give me. What I wish is, to see a black-robe pour water on my brother's head, and speak the words which would make him a Christian.'

' The chief of prayer is no more. I have sung his death-song in my heart. He can never again speak to the living.'

' But there are other black-robes—other chiefs of prayer? '

' They must all be killed by this time. Think no more of them, little dove of the white man's tribe, and speak not to Ontara of the French prayer. He is a child of the Sun, and worships his father.'

'But I know he carries a crucifix in his bosom,' Mina eagerly cried, pointing to the Indian's breast.

'My father, Outalissi, gave it me; and for his sake I keep it close to my heart.'

At that moment Osseo joined them. Mina was not afraid of him when her new brother was by her side. He was much excited, and cried out, as soon as he saw them:

'I have discovered the fetish which the great sorcerer of the Abnakis possessed. He told me of it some time ago, and I have been searching for it ever since.'

'What is it?' Ontara asked.

Osseo drew a small serpent from his bosom: 'I have charmed it to sleep,' he said, as Mina drew back affrighted. 'It will not wake till I bid it. This fetish is so powerful that he who owns it never shoots an arrow in vain, and is never conquered in battle; and when he goes out hunting he brings home more game than any one else.'

'Throw it away, Osseo; throw it away,' Mina exclaimed. 'It will do you no good.'

'And if I throw it away,' said the youth,

with a sneer, 'will the dove of the white tribe nestle in my bosom?'

'I will love you very much,' Mina answered, fixing her large bright eyes on the young savage.

'Not so much as Ontara?' said Osseo, with a malignant glance at the young chief.

'Ontara is my brother,' Mina answered, drawing closer to her protector.

'And if anyone dares to touch a single hair of her head,' cried Ontara, 'I will take him before the sachems, and slay him where he stands.'

A dark hue overspread the face of the other youth; but he made no direct reply. Stroking the serpent in his bosom, he said to the little girl: 'When five summers have come and gone, you shall choose which of us you will marry.'

'I will not marry you, and I cannot marry him,' Mina answered, with simplicity.

'Why not?' said Ontara, quickly. 'You are no longer a slave, since you have become my sister; and when you are old enough we shall stand before the sachems, in the presence of the Great Sun, and I will make you my wife.'

Mina shook her head : 'The daughters of the white men, her parents said, did not marry the sons of other tribes.'

'Then you will never marry at all,' Osseo fiercely cried. 'There will not be a single white man left to be your husband. The Indians will kill them all.'

'No,' Mina answered ; 'the great God will not let them do it. He is more powerful than all your fetishes.'

'But not than the glorious orb which the Natches adore,' said Ontara, pointing to the sun, at that moment setting in a bed of fiery clouds.

'The God of the Christians made the sun, and the moon, and the stars,' Mina replied, and then she sat down with the two Indians on the grass by the well-side, and they talked of the Natches' worship and the Christian prayer. A child's simple conceptions of religion were more adapted to the comprehension of these uncultivated minds than the teachings of older persons. They listened eagerly to her words. Each of them had fastened, as it were, on the side of their false belief which was most in harmony with their

natural tendencies. Osseo's mind was filled
with the gloomy superstitions of devil-wor-
ship. His faith in spells and charms was
unbounded. He had studied the secrets of
magic under the most learned soothsayers
of the neighbouring tribes, and was an
adept in all the arts of witchcraft. Ontara,
on the contrary—perhaps from an instinctive
preference of light to darkness, and also on
account of his close relationship to the representative of the orb of day—yielded a peculiar and exclusive homage to the sun. It
seemed to him to embody all the ideas he
had ever formed of brightness and majesty.
At morn he hailed its rising, at noon he
prostrated himself in adoration before its
dazzling beams, and saluted its setting with
hymns of praise. Mina drew from her
pocket a prayer-book, and read to the wor-
shipper of the sun these verses of the
Psalms:

' " The heavens show forth the glory of
God : and the firmament declareth the work
of his hands.

' " Day to day uttereth speech : and night
to night showeth knowledge.

' " There are no speeches nor languages where their voices are not heard.

' " Their sound has gone forth into all the earth : and their words unto the ends of the world.

' " He hath set his tabernacle in the sun : and he, as a bridegroom coming out of his bride-chamber, hath rejoiced as a giant to run his way.

' " His going out is from the end of heaven, and his circuit even to the end thereof : and there is no one that can hide himself from his heat." '

Ontara listened attentively to her artless translation of the sublime words of holy writ, and made her repeat it till he learned the verses by heart. Osseo caressed the serpent in his bosom, and said he would belong to the Christian prayer if it had more powerful charms than those of the Abnakis.

'When my arm has acquired its full strength,' he exultingly declared, 'and my fetish its full growth, my name will become as famous as that of the great Oneyda, or of the wise Hiawatha, the Son of the West Wind.'

A sign from her mother recalled Mina to the palace; Madame d'Auban was patiently listening to Madame Lenoir's account of the sad manner in which one of her gowns had been cut up to fit it for an Indian woman. If it had been an act of charity to fill her pitcher, it was a greater one still to let her talk of the dresses she had brought from Paris. It comforted her more than anything else could have done, and she went back to her hard duties soothed, as she declared, by Madame d'Auban's sympathy in her trials.

CHAPTER III.

And were not these high words to flow
  From woman's breaking heart ?
Through all that night of bitterest woe
  She bore her lofty part.

The wind rose high ; but with it rose
  Her voice, that they might hear ;
Perchance that dark hour brought repose
  To careless bosoms near.
While she stood striving with despair,

  .   .   .   .   .   .

And pouring her deep soul in prayer
  Forth on the rushing storm.
                              Mrs. Hemans.

ANOTHER day elapsed, and another ; and each
time that the sun set without any change
taking place, or any rumour of help from
without cheering the captives' ears, it became
harder for them to struggle against despair.

'Mother,' Mina said at last, as she threw
her arms round Madame d'Auban's neck,
'may I go and look for my father? Let
me slip out of the hut at night when nobody
will miss me, and go to the country of the

Choktaws, on the other side of the river. I
am sure he is there.'

'Why do you think so, Mina?' eagerly
asked her mother, whose head had been
drooping on her breast in heavy despondency,
whose eyes were strained with watching, and
whose ears had grown dull by the continual
effort to catch a sound which might indicate
the approach of the French.

'My brother Ontara says so. He has seen
a man who told him that a white chief was
raising a war-cry amongst the Choktaws, and
that they are taking up arms. He will row
me across the river if I can get away when
it is dark, because he promised to do whatever I asked him; and he says a child of the
sun always keeps his promises. He will show
me which way to take, and in what direction
to go. He cannot smoke the calumet to the
Choktaws, because they are enemies of the
Natches; but I am sure I shall find my father,
and I will bring him back with me, mother.'

'They watch us too closely, Mina. You
know that our taskmistress sleeps with her
back to the door of the hut, to prevent any
chance of our getting away. I could not let

you go alone, my child; but if this young
Indian is indeed willing to favour our escape,
I should be inclined to accept his aid.'

'Ah! mother, they will not let us leave
the hut; but there is a space between the
planks just behind our mat, which I have
been enlarging with my fingers, and by lying
quite flat on the ground I think I could creep
out, if you would give me leave.'

Madame d'Auban shuddered, and threw
her arms round her child. 'Mina!' she
exclaimed with agitation, 'promise me not
to stir from my side. I forbid you to think
of leaving me—not at present, at least. I
must tell you, my child, that a great danger
hangs over us. That poor foolish Madame
Lenoir has been making a plot with the
black slaves against our Indian masters. It
cannot succeed, and if it is discovered we
shall be probably all doomed to death. If
the worst comes to the worst, I may bid you
fly alone. I do not think they would kill
you, but to leave you in their hands without
me would be worse than death. Better that
you should perish in the woods seeking your
father than grow up amongst these savages

Mina, I may not have an opportunity of speaking to you again   One thing I have to say to you, which you must remember as long as you live.   You are a Christian, and the child of European parents.   You must never abandon your faith, and you must never marry an Indian.'

Mina slipt off her mother's knees and stood before her, clasping her hands together.

'Then I shall never marry at all, mother, for I told Ontara that I could not be his wife, because you say that white girls must not marry their Indian brothers.   But I also promised him that I would never marry a white man.'

'That was foolish, my child,' answered her mother.   'You are too young to make such promises.   They mean nothing.'

'Mother, I am sure I shall keep that promise.   I am sure it meant something.'

Madame d'Auban felt annoyed at the little girl's earnestness, even though she tried to treat it as mere childishness.   It was in keeping with the passionate affection she had always shown for the land of her birth and its native inhabitants.

'If I were to die, Mina, and you remained alone in this country, what would you do?'

'I would remember all you have taught me, mother, and I would try to be good.'

'And if they tried to make you a heathen, like themselves?'

'They should kill me first.'

There was at that moment in the child's face and manner so strong a resemblance to her father, that it took her poor mother by surprise. She bowed her head on her little daughter's bosom, as if seeking for support in that terrible hour from the brave heart in that child's breast.

Clasping each other in a mute embrace, they remained silent for an instant, and then Madame Lenoir came running towards them in wild affright.

'It is all over with us,' she gasped out in an agonised whisper. 'It was such a beautiful plot! and to think it should not have succeeded after all!' And she wrung her hands and lifted up her eyes, without attending to Madame d'Auban's anxious questions.

'Has it merely failed? or has it been discovered?' she tremblingly asked.

'Discovered! Yes, of course it has been discovered. One of those wretched negroes has betrayed us, and now we shall all be put to death. Oh! that it should have come to this, such a beautiful plot as it was! It put me in mind of the Conjuration de Cinna at the Théâtre Français. The traitor! the black monster! the wretch! . . . Madame d'Auban, you are like a statue, like a stone; you feel nothing.'

'For God's sake, be silent; give me time to think,' said Mina's mother, pressing her hands to her brow. She remained motionless awhile, and when she lifted up her eyes Ontara was standing before her. He was speaking in a low, rapid manner, with various gesticulations, to Mina.

'What does he say?' asked her mother, who did not well understand the Natches' language.

'He says that at midnight all the white women and children will be taken to the square in the middle of the village, and each tied there to a stake, and at sunrise they will burn them to death. He asked the Sun, his father, not to kill me, because I was his little sister, and that he loves me, but the Sun will not listen to him, and says the white-skins must all die. And I do not want to live, if they kill you, mother.' She threw herself into her arms, and sobbed on her bosom. ' But, oh! what will my father do?'

Again Ontara spoke urgently to the weeping child.

' What does he say? What does he say?' asked the distracted mother.

' He says if I will creep out of the hut through that hole to-night, before they carry us away to the square, that he will wait for me outside, and take me to his boat and across the river to the land of the Choktaws.'

Madame d'Auban raised her heart to Heaven for help and for guidance. It was a dreadful moment. The agony of that decision was almost unbearable. She fixed her eyes with a wild, imploring expression on the young Indian's face. He seemed to understand the mute question, the imploring appeal. Quickly he drew the crucifix from his breast, made the gesture which according to Indian custom signifies an oath, and laid his hand on Mina's head.

Madame d'Auban knew that this meant a solemn promise of protection. She had seen that the boy had a good heart and a noble spirit. She instinctively found words in which to express, in a way he partly understood, that she would trust him; and Mina clung to her, and said, 'Mother, do not be afraid; Ontara is good, and I will bring back my father in time to save you.'

The shades of evening had fallen; the deepest silence reigned in the hut, where the captives and their Indian companions were reposing. Repose—strange word for such an hour of mortal agony as one of those human beings was enduring, as she lay motionless on the mat with her child by her side! She clasped her hand in her own, as if to make sure she was not gone; but go she must, for the words which Ontara had spoken were true, and the doom of the captives had been pronounced. A reckless woman's fatal imprudence had done its work, and the whole tribe of the Natches risen in wild fury. They would have slain their victims at once, had it not been that they rejoiced in the anticipation of their protracted sufferings. Already the European and negro slaves were being dragged from the huts of their masters, and led to the centre of the village, where the sachems were assembled. The Indians were brandishing their tomahawks, erecting stakes, and carrying ropes wherewith to bind their victims. The tramp of their feet, the sounds of wailing from the women, and the cries of children, were heard in the portion of the palace where Madame d'Auban was confined. She felt there was no time to lose. Her lips were pressed close to Mina's ear. 'My child,' she whispered, 'the time is come when I must trust you to God and to your guardian angel. Remember, my daughter, your mother's last words. Do not cry, my own; the least sob might be heard. Be always good, Mina, and the Blessed Virgin will be thy mother. God bless thee, dearest! Now, creep away; God bless thee; God guide thee!' One long, silent, ardent, passionate embrace, and then, by the light of the moon shining through the planks of the hut, the mother watched the child gliding out through the narrow opening in its wall.

She was gone. Gone whither? gone with whom?—a young savage for her guide. Had she been mad, to part with her thus? Her heart almost ceased to beat. She stretched herself on the ground near the opening through which the child had passed, and gazed on the meadow illumined by the brilliant moonlight. Distinctly she discerned Mina's figure bounding over the dewy grass with the swiftness of a young antelope, and keeping pace with the Indian, who had joined her. The two forms on which her strained eyes were gazing, disappeared from her sight. They plunged into the thickets which led to the river. She turned round and hid her face in the heap of dried leaves on which the child's head had rested a moment before, to stifle the least sound from passing her lips, to still, by a strong effort, the agony which was convulsing her frame.

It was almost a relief when they came to fetch her away from the hut. No great search was made for Mina. The woman who was set to guard the captives said a few words to the messengers, which apparently accounted for her absence. She made a

show of zeal, however, by showering re-
proaches on Madame d'Auban, and dragging
her roughly to the door of the hut.   To the
mother's heart ill-usage was welcome ; the
sight of the stakes to which women and
children were being bound, the cruelty of
the Indians, their savage glee, a strange sort
of consolation.   Had her own life been
spared, the thought that she had sent her
child unguarded, save by her Indian playmate, into the wilderness, would have mad-
dened her.   Now that she was herself about
to die, she felt she could commit her without
reserve to God's protection ; now she could
murmur with intense gratitude, 'She is gone,
she is gone ; ' and her mental vision fixed
itself with an intensity which was almost
like sight on the thought of the crucifix on
the breast of her young guide.   Through the
long hours of that terrible night, the Christian
heroine bore her lofty part, and during the
next dreadful day, and when the shades of
evening fell, and again through the night,
which was to be the last to so many human
beings doomed to perish at sunrise — in
the full light of the glorious, majestic sun,

the noblest of God's inanimate works, the object of idolatrous worship to the heathen murderers gathered around them, the silent witness of men's errors and men's crimes. She forgot herself; she forgot her absent husband and her fugitive child, in the intense, all-absorbing desire to prepare for death and judgment her companions in adversity; she found strength to raise her voice and speak of hope to the perishing, of pardon to the guilty. She repeated aloud acts of faith, of love, and of contrition; she said that Mary was praying and Jesus waiting; that one word, one sigh, one upward glance was enough to win heaven in that hour; and as the Indians danced, as was their wont, around their victims, and made the air resound with their songs of savage glee, her voice still rose above their discordant cries, her prayers filled up every pause in their dreadful merriment, and grace was given her to do an angel's work in the midst of those breaking hearts and those infuriated men.

The remaining hours of life were waning fast. The prisoners were to die at sunrise, and the first faint light of morning was beginning

to dawn in the sky. Many of the Indians set
to guard the prisoners, who were, however,
tightly bound to their respective stakes, had
fallen asleep, having largely indulged throughout the night in the 'fiery essence,' as they
called brandy, which they had brought away
in great quantities from the French fort.
Madame d'Auban was still speaking, in a
feeble, exhausted manner, to poor Madame
Lenoir, whose cries of despair had subsided
into weary groans, when she heard a voice
close behind her, and turning round, as much
as the ropes with which she was bound
allowed, she saw Osseo, with a knife in his
hand, standing half concealed from sight.

'Daughter of the white man,' he whispered,
'Where is Mina? I will cut these ropes
and show thee how to escape whilst these
men sleep, if thou wilt tell me where I can
find her.'

'The Great Spirit alone knows where she
is now,' answered Madame d'Auban, shudder-
at the expression of Osseo's face.

'Do not talk to me of the Great Spirit, or
of your detested prayer. I want Mina; and
I have in my bosom a fetish which will help

me to find her, if thou dost refuse to tell me where she is, and thou art going to die.' He added, in a mocking tone, ' The fire is even now being kindled which will shrivel thy white limbs, as the flame burns up the wood of the forest. Tell me where Mina is, and I will save thee.'

Madame d'Auban feebly shook her head; her strength was quite exhausted.

' I will search for her all over the land,' the young savage cried, brandishing a tomahawk ; ' and if thou hast sent her across the great salt lake, I can row a swifter boat than man has ever yet made.'

The mother closed her eyes, and heard the sound of his retreating steps ; and then for a while the silence was unbroken, save by the groans of the prisoners and the heavy snoring of their drunken foes.

The next time she opened her eyes the sun was illuminating the mountain tops.

' Glorious orb of day ! harbinger of death,' she murmured. ' Blessed be thy light shining on our painful way to heaven ! Blessed be thy rays warming our limbs, as the love of Jesus warms our hearts ! Dark-

ness is still brooding over the plain, but the
heights are even now resplendent with light;
the shadows of death at hand, the glory of
heaven shining beyond them. O my God!
Thou dost, indeed, send thy messenger before
Thee! My beloved ones, farewell!'

Her head fell on her breast; she neither
moved nor spoke, but silently prepared for
death. Hark! what was the sound which
fell upon her ear, like the splash of rain-
drops on the leaves of the forest, like the
footfall of watchers near a dying man's bed?
Can a band of armed men tread so lightly?
Can a troop of warriors steal along with so
noiseless a progress? Yes, for they are of
the swift, light-footed tribe of the Choktaws.
They are the deep divers, the wily hunters
of the Western Prairies. They track the
wild beast to his den, and surprise the
alligator in his sleep by the river side. And
they have listened to the white man's appeal.
In their own tongue they have heard him
tell his dreadful tale. There has been a
long hereditary feud between them and the
children of the Sun, and their hatred of the
Natches has kindled into a flame, on hearing

of the murder of the black-robe; for the
Père Souël had been amongst them and
spoken of ' the prayer of the Christians,' and
they had answered, 'It is well; we have
heard your words, and we will think on
what you tell us.' At the voice of the
stranger they have risen as one man. Seven
hundred warriors performed the dance of
war, and pledged themselves to the rescue
of the white men's wives and children.
From the villages and the solitary wigwams,
from the hills and from the plains, they
emerged and joined the white leader, and
crossed the great river by the light of the
crescent moon. As the day dawns in the
east they draw near to the City of the Sun.
In silence they advance. If they speak, it
is under their breath. D'Auban marches at
the head of the red warriors, the only
stranger amongst them — the only one for
whom more than life or than fame is at
stake. He feels in himself the strength to
struggle with a thousand foes, and yet the
stirring of a leaf makes his heart beat like
a woman's. It was such a terrible suspense
—such an agonising uncertainty! His eyes

strive to pierce the dewy mist which hides
from him the distant view. They grow dim
with straining, those burning, tearless eyes,
and the tangled boughs and the feathery
branches of the forest take odd, fantastic
shapes, which mock his yearning sight. In
the dim vista of an opening in the wood he
fancies that he sees two figures advance.
No; one is advancing and the other recedes,
and after a while disappears. But that
something white which approaches, what is
it? Is the mist thickening, or his sight
failing? He can discern nothing. But
a voice, a cry, reaches his ear. 'Father!
Oh, Father!' He rushes forward, and Mina
is in his arms. The band of warriors gathers
round them.

'Your mother? Where is your mother?'

'She sent me away; I crept out of the
hut. Make haste; make haste!'

'Is she safe? Is she well? How have
they treated you?'

'Well, till last night. Make haste, father;
make haste! The sachems were very angry
when my mother sent me away.'

D'Auban took up his little daughter in his

arms as if she had weighed but a feather, and strode forward. He could have carried three times her weight and not have felt it, so intensely strained was his nervous system. But, suddenly halting, he turned to the Indians and said—'My brothers, the Great Spirit has sent this child to meet us. The Great Spirit is with us, and will bless my Indian brothers for the deed they do this day.'

A whisper went through the warriors' ranks.

'The white maiden,' they said, ' was come from the Great Spirit to lead them to the City of the Sun;' and onward they pressed through the tangled thickets, grasping their weapons like the hunter who discerns the footsteps of his prey.

The wood is passed at last, and the open plain lies stretched before them. They see the white wigwams of the Natches' city amongst the oleander and acacia groves. Another hour's march and they will have reached it. D'Auban calls one of the Indians.

' My brother Pearl Feather,' he says, 'take this child, and stay with her in this spot. If

we succeed we will send for you from yonder
city, to sing with us the song of victory ; but if
the night comes and no tidings reach you, then
say " My white brother is dead," and take
the child to the black robe of the nearest
mission, or to the French in the south,
and the Great Spirit will bless thee, my
brother, and show thee the way to the land
of the hereafter.'

'I will not leave you, father,' Mina cried,
convulsively grasping her father's arm ; 'let
me run by your side. I could keep up with
Ontara, let me stay with you.'

'Mina, in God's name, and as your father,
I command you to remain here.' He had
spoken as if in anger, and the child flung
herself on the ground in a paroxysm of grief.
He did not trust himself to look back. He
went on, for every minute was a matter of
life and death ; and the fair-haired child remained lying on the greensward motionless
as a marble image, pale as a broken lily,
refusing to be comforted by the Indian, who
tried in vain to direct her thoughts to other
objects than the onward march of that little

band towards the city where the lives of both her parents were hanging on a thread.

The hour had arrived when the sachems were to assemble in the square to witness the execution of the European captives. The gong which was to summon them was to have sounded when the sun rose, but the sleeping guards awoke from their drunken slumbers to witness a far different scene. Weapons were brandished in their eyes and over their heads. Flames were bursting forth from various buildings in the town. The wigwams were set on fire in every direction, and d'Auban's warriors had encircled the square, whilst he rushed to the stakes and cut the cords which bound the prisoners.

A cry of rage and terror arose from the affrighted city. The whilom triumphant Natches now rent the air with their howls of fury. They rushed about in wild confusion, some to oppose their enemies, the number of which they could not discern, so utter had been the surprise, so swift and stealthy their approach,—some to extinguish the flames which were extending over the village, and threatened the chief's palace.

D'Auban had caught his wife in his arms just as she was sinking to the ground. 'Mina?' she had just strength to murmur.

'She is safe,' he answered, 'Bear up for a while, my beloved one. The lives of all these helpless ones depend on the event of this hour.' Then assuming the direction of the assailing force, he assigned to a hundred men the task of conveying the women and children to the shore, where boats had been previously sent to await them. He despatched a man to the spot where he had left his child under the care of her Indian protector, with orders to proceed at once to the river side. With his remaining force he kept the enemy engaged, and dreadful was the fierce encounter between the two tribes. Many a Natchez fell under the blows of the more warlike Choktaws; but the struggle was an unequal one, and if prolonged must have turned to the advantage of the Children of the Sun, who were beginning to recover from their surprise and hurrying from every side to join the conflict. D'Auban's superior military skill enabled him to conduct the retreat of his band, and to cope successfully with their far more numerous pursuers. He had sent a messenger to Fort Rosalie, and had hoped that a French force might have been despatched in time to meet him; but a keen-eyed Indian who surveyed the country from one of the neighbouring heights could discern no sign of their approach, and he determined on effecting if possible the rescue of the captives without attempting to maintain their position in the Natches' city, which they had, as it were, taken by storm. The Choktaw Indians, like the Parthians of old, discharged their arrows at their enemies as they retreated, and d'Auban with the musket which had already done him such good service kept them also at bay. At the sight of the murderous weapon the pursuers fell back. Their missiles made havoc the while amongst the rescuing party, and many a Choktaw warrior remained stark and cold on the green slopes between the City of the Sun and the Father of Waters. At last the shore was reached, and whilst the gallant band under d'Auban's command faced the foe, the women and children were embarked in the boats and barges manned with rowers of the friendly tribe.

Madame d'Auban's face turned as pale as ashes, for Mina was nowhere to be seen. Boat after boat was filled with women and children, and shot down the stream, impelled by the rowers and aided by the current. But one remained. D'Auban and his Indians fought on ; but how long would they remain by his side ? How long were they to wait ? How long would they shed their blood for the sake of that one missing child ? Himself he felt his strength giving way, his arm waxing weak, his head growing dizzy. At that moment the sky was lighted up by a lurid glare. The Natches looked back towards their homes, and saw the flames bursting out afresh from every grove and every temple of the City of the Sun. A cry rose to their lips ; abandoning in tumultuous haste the pursuit, they retraced their steps, and rushed wildly back towards the burning town. At that moment also, staggering under a burden that was no longer a light one for the dying man who was bearing it, Pearl Feather, the swiftest runner of his tribe, fell breathless at d'Auban's feet. Mina was in her father's arms, and the Indian gasped out in feeble accents, 'The bird of prey sought to carry away the dove, and his fetish has great power. But the Great Spirit of the Christian prayer was more powerful still. He gave me strength to bring her to thee, my white brother, and now depart and leave me to die.'

Then d'Auban saw the arrow which was lodged in the Indian's breast, and guessed it was a poisoned one. For one moment he knelt by the true friend who had saved his child; and when the brave spirit passed away, the prayers and the blessing which followed it beyond this mortal scene were of those which are not spoken in words, but rise straight from the heart with speechless intensity.

The friendly Indians for the most part swam across the river and dispersed in the woods, bearing away with them as much as they could carry of the treasures stolen from the city during their brief invasion of its precincts. The barge which held d'Auban, his wife and child, the corpse of her dead deliverer, and a few of their companions in the late combat, descended the river with all the swiftness possible under

the circumstances. It was a wonderful escape
the captives had had, and Mina's, perhaps, the
most wonderful of all.   Osseo had met her
and her protector on the way to the river,
and sought to detain the white maiden, who,
he said, was a runaway slave from the chief's
palace, and force her back to the town. Most
likely he would have succeeded, for his
strength was superior to that of an old man
and a child, had not Ontara, who was also
searching for Mina in every direction, arrived
on the spot at that very moment and taken
part with the fugitives.   Osseo turned with
fury on his new opponent, which gave the
Indian time to fly with the little girl in his
arms.   Like an arrow from a bow, swiftly
and straightly he crossed the plain, through
the feathery grasses and waving fields of
green maize.   Already were the armed men
on the river side and their boats there
in sight, when a shaft, a poisoned one
too, came whizzing through the air and
struck him as he ran.   No cry escaped his
lips ; he scarcely slackened his pace: but the
child he was carrying felt he was wounded,
and that his steps were faltering.   She shut

her eyes in anguish and called to him to stop,
but he heeded her not ; his lips faintly murmured a chant which was the death song of
his tribe, but the words he set to it were
those of the Christian prayer. His blood
coloured the greensward up to the margin
of the stream. He died silently at the feet
of the friend whose child he had saved.
No wonder that burning tears of gratitude
and of sorrow fell on the lifeless form of the
Indian, as he lay stiff and cold at the bottom
of the boat which bore away the captives to
safety and to freedom.

Three days afterwards sheltering walls
enclosed the weary fugitives, and the call
of French sentries, as they paced around the
fort which had received them, sounded like
music in their ears. D'Auban sat between
his wife and child, looking at them with a
tenderness too deep for words. He was
beginning to feel the effects of the intense
fatigue and excitement he had gone through.
His weary limbs and overwrought mind were
sinking with exhaustion. He was become
grey-haired, and looked ten years older than
when he had left St. Agathe. His wife

recovered more quickly. At her age there is still an elasticity of spirits, which surmounts more speedily the effects of suffering than at a more advanced period of life; and though she had borne much anguish, she had not had, like him, to act under its intolerable pressure.

When Mina went to bed that evening she hid her face in the pillow, but her parents heard her sobbing as if her heart would break.

'What ails you, my child?' her mother tenderly inquired, whilst her father anxiously bent over her.

'I shall never see my brother again,' cried the weeping child. 'He has saved my life, and I love him better than any one in the world, except you both. I heard one of the soldiers say that the French were marching to the Natches' city, and would kill all its inhabitants. O father, they will kill my brother, who saved your life and mine!'

D'Auban was much affected at this thought, and at his daughter's well-founded fears. He assured her that as soon as they reached

New Orleans he would go to the governor,
and entreat him to send orders to the
commandant of the French troops to save
the life of the young chief Ontara, and to
treat him with kindness.

'Let us go on at once, then,' cried Mina,
sitting up in her bed.

'We shall start to-morrow morning,' said
her mother. 'Try and sleep, my child.'

It was some days, however, before d'Auban
recovered sufficiently to leave Bâton Rouge;
but he sent a letter to M. Perrier by one of
the soldiers of the fort. He felt great misgivings about the young Indian's fate, though
he tried to calm Mina's fears and to divert
her mind from the subject. If he had
grown old in the space of a few days, his
little girl had become almost a woman in
thought and feeling during the same lapse of
time. She did not play any more. Her
mind was incessantly going over the past,
or forming plans for the future, with an
intense imaginative power which hastened in
some respects the development of her character. The scenes she had gone through;
the memories they had left behind them;

the sight of her father's enfeebled frame, and of the anxious looks her mother bent upon him; the uncertainty in which Ontara's fate was involved,—had a depressing effect on her affectionate and highly sensitive temperament. It was an abrupt transition from a life as joyous and as free as a child had ever led, to one too full of cares and conflicting feelings for one so young and so naturally thoughtful. As her spirits did not revive after their arrival at New Orleans, her parents resolved to place her for a while at the school of the Ursuline Convent, in the hope that regular habits of study and the society of girls of her own age would dissipate the depressing effects of the scenes she had witnessed. The results of this experiment were not at first very successful.

CHAPTER IV.

In the cruel fire of sorrow
Cast thy heart, do not faint or wail,
Let thy hand be firm and steady,
Do not let thy spirits quail.
But wait till the time is over,
And take thy heart again ;
For as gold is tried by fire,
So a heart must be tried by pain.
Adelaide Proctor.

A thousand thoughts of all things dear,
Like shadows o'er me sweep ;
I leave my sunny childhood here ;
Oh ! therefore, let me weep.
Mrs. Hemans.

ABOUT three months after the events related in the last chapter, a number of girls of various ages were playing amongst the orange trees of the garden of the Ursuline Convent, with all the vivacity belonging to youth and the French character. They had just obtained a holiday in honour of the news which had reached New Orleans, of the final suppression of the Natches insurrection by a body of French troops, and

their patriotic exultation was at its height.
A handsome, clever-looking girl of fifteen
jumped upon a bench, under a banana tree,
and began to harangue the crowd which
gathered round her. Emilie de Beauregard
was a great favourite in the school, and before she opened her mouth the girls clapped
their hands, and then cried out ' Silence ! '

' Mesdemoiselles !' she began, ' let your
French hearts rejoice! Your countrymen
have gained a glorious victory! The royal
flag, the white lilies of France, floats over the
ruins of the city of the Sun.' A round of
applause saluted this exordium. The orator,
warmed by success, went on. ' The frus-
trated enemy bites the dust. They dared to
kill Frenchmen; but now vengeance has over-
taken them, and the rivers run with their
blood.'

' That was in our historical lesson this
morning,' whispered Julie d'Artaban to Rose
Perrier.

' Never mind. Hold your tongue,' answered
the governor's daughter. ' It is very fine.'

' The houses of those monsters are a
prey to the flames—not a corn-field or an

orange garden remains in the plain where French blood has been spilt. These Indians are all as cruel as wild beasts, but now they are hunted down without mercy. Their princes, the Children of the Sun, as they call themselves, are all slain or sold away as slaves. Not one of their dark visages will ever be seen again in the land of their birth.'

This was too much for one of the audience. There was a sudden rush to the bench. Mina d'Auban, with flashing eyes and crimson cheeks, had seized and overturned it, and the orator had fallen full length on the grass. This assault naturally enough made Mdlle. de Beauregard very angry, and her friends and admirers still more so. Cries of ' You naughty girl ! ' ' You wicked Indian princess !' (this was Mina's nickname in the school), resounded on every side.

' Fi donc ! Mademoiselle,' exclaimed Julie d'Artaban ; and Rose Perrier, who had high ideas of administrative justice, ran to call Sister Gertrude, the mistress of the class.

The placid-looking nun found Mina crying in the midst of her excited and indignant companions, who all bore witness to the outrage she had committed.

'She pushed Emilie down because she was telling us the good news that the French have won a great victory.'

'It is impossible to play with Mademoiselle d'Auban,' said another. 'She flies into a passion if we say we like our own country people better than Indians and negroes.'

'She said all the Indians are monsters,' said Mina, sobbing; 'and I think she is a monster herself to say so. Some of them are very good—better than white people.' There was a general burst of laughter, which increased her exasperation, and she passionately exclaimed, 'I hate white people!'

'Come with me, my child,' said Sister Gertrude; 'you do not know what you are saying. You must not remain with your companions if you cannot control your temper. Go and sit in the school-room alone for an hour, and I will speak to you afterwards.'

Poor Mina's heart was bursting with grief and indignation; and her conscience also reproached her for her violence. She could not bring herself to forgive her companions, or to feel at peace with them. This conflict

had been going on ever since she had been
at school. The separation from her parents
had been a hard trial. They had thought
that the companionship of French children
would divert her mind from painful thoughts,
and overcome her determined predilection
for the Indians. But they had not calculated
on the effect produced upon her by the
unmitigated abhorrence her playmates expressed for the people she so dearly loved.
Their hatred made no distinction between
the treacherous Natches and the good Illinois
Christians ; and a rankling sense of injustice
kept up her irritation. It was, perhaps, as
natural that these girls, most of whom had lost
friends and relations in the insurrection, should
feel an antipathy for the Indians, as that Mina,
with all her recollections of St. Agathe, and
her gratitude and affection for Ontara and for
Pearl Feather, should resent its expression.

But the result was, that instead of dimi-
nishing her overweening partiality for the
land of her birth and its native inhabitants,
her residence at school had hitherto only
served to increase it. She also sadly missed
the freedom of her earlier years. She was

often in disgrace for breaches of discipline. The confinement of the class-room was trying to her; and she committed faults of a peculiar nature, such as taking off her stockings in order to cross barefooted the little stream which ran through the garden, and climbing up the trees to get a glimpse of the sea, the sight of which reminded her of the green waving fields of her home.

When Sister Gertrude entered the school-room she found her at first silent and sad, but by degrees her gentle manner and soothing words drew from the overburthened heart of the poor child the expression of her feelings; she understood them, and while blaming her violence, she made allowance for the provocation, and showed sympathy in the trial she was enduring. It was not only at school that Mina's sensitive nature was wounded by the absence of such sympathy: her father and mother had suffered so terribly during the days of her captivity, and of his absence, that they involuntarily shrunk from everything which reminded them of that time. They would have made every effort and every sacrifice in their power for

the sake of the young Indian who had pro-
tected their child, and prayed daily for the
brave man who had died to save her. But
the mention of their names recalled such
terrible scenes that they instinctively recoiled
from it. Mina perceived this without quite
understanding it. She had the quick tact to
feel that though she was never told not to
speak of them, the subject was evidently not a
welcome one ; and nobody could have guessed
how much the child suffered from this tacit
prohibition. St. Agathe, too, was not often
alluded to by her parents. When she spoke
of that beloved place, her mother looked
sad and anxious. She watched her husband's looks with daily increasing anxiety.
Yearnings for his native country, the home-
sickness which sometimes so suddenly seizes
exiles, joined to the early stages of a disease
brought on by violent bodily exertions and
mental anxiety, had greatly affected Colonel
d'Auban's spirits, and Mina could not pour
forth her thoughts in his presence with the
same freedom she had been used to do. Nothing had been discovered as to Ontara's
fate. Every inquiry had been made by

d'Auban regarding the royal family of the
Natches. He ascertained what had become
of all its members except the two young
men, Ontara and Osseo. They had either
perished or taken refuge amongst some of
the more distant tribes. A reward was promised for their capture, as it was deemed
dangerous to allow any of the relatives of
the great Sun to remain at liberty. But, at
his friends' earnest entreaty, the governor
gave orders, that if Ontara was arrested, he
should be treated with kindness and instantly
brought to New Orleans.

It was a great consolation to Mina to relate
all her story to Sister Gertrude on the day
when matters had arrived at a crisis between
her and her companions.

'You see, dear sister,' she said, ' I am an
Indian girl, though my skin is white. I was
born in the Illinois ; and I only wish I was
brown, and had black eyes and hair like my
own people.'

' But, my dear, that is not right. You are
a creole, not an Indian. Your parents are
French, and you ought to be glad that you
are like them.'

' And so I should be, sister, if the white girls loved the Indians ; but they hate them, and I then want them to hate me also.'

' But what a shocking word that is for Christians to use ! I do not think your companions really hate these poor people. I am sure I hope not, for we are going to receive here to-morrow six little native orphan girls whose parents were killed in the insurrection. They were to have been sold as slaves, but our good mother begged them of the Company, and we are going to bring them up as Christians. This evening, after night prayers, I shall say a few words to our children, and tell them that for the love of Christ they should welcome and cherish these little outcasts. But Mina, my child, you should also remember that Anna Mirepoix's father, and Jeanne Castel's brother, and Virginia d'Aumont's uncle have all died by the hand of the red men ; and when they say things which make you angry, ask yourself what you would have felt if your father had been murdered and your mother burnt to death in the city of the Natches.'

Mina threw herself into Sister Gertrude's

arms, and shed tears of repentance for her
fault, and of joy that the little brown
orphans were coming to a sheltering roof.
From that day a new era began in her
school life. The nuns had rightly judged
that the best way of softening their pupils'
feelings towards the unfortunate natives
was to appeal to their pity, and enlist
their sympathy in behalf of the orphans.
The experiment proved successful. A few
days after the one on which Emilie de Beauregard had tumbled off the bench in the
midst of her harangue, she was sitting upon it
with a brown baby on her lap, whilst Mina,
kneeling before her, was amusing it with a
bunch of feathers. Rose Perrier and Julie
d'Artaban were quarrelling for the possession
of another. All the girls were making Mina
teach them Indian words, that they might
know how to talk to the little savages, who
became quite the fashion in the school. As
to Mina, she was a mother to them all; the
tiny creatures clung to her with an instinctive
affection. During her lessons they would
sit silent and motionless at her feet, with the
patience which even in childhood belongs to

their race, and followed her about the garden
in the hours of recreation like a pack of little
dogs. Every sweetmeat given to her was
made over to them, and the only presents
she valued were clothes or toys for her infant
charges. Her health and spirits rapidly
improved under this change of circumstances.
She grew very fast, and was not very strong;
but her colour returned, and bright smiles
were again seen on her lovely face.

There are persons whose destiny it seems
to have no lasting abode on earth; scattered
workers, may be, or busy idlers, who, during
the whole course of their lives, pass from one
place to another, as if the wanderer's doom
had been pronounced upon them. The
place of their birth knows them no more.
The homes of their childhood, the haunts of
their youth, they never revisit. Every local
attachment they form is blighted in the bud.
The curtain drops on each successive scene
of their pilgrimage, and *finis* is stamped on
almost every page of their existence. Some
call this a strange fatality; others see in it, in
particular instances, the hand of God's Providence training particular souls to detachment

and self-sacrifice. 'Le Chrétien est-il d'aucun
lieu?' asks Emilie de Guérin, who was a
genius, and perhaps a saint too, without
knowing it.

Thoughts such as these, though scarcely
put into shape, but vaguely floating through
the mind, crossed Madame d'Auban, as she
sat one evening planning with her husband
the future course of their lives. It was
almost determined between them that they
should go to France. Many a sleepless
night, many an hour of anxious thought,
had she spent before making up her mind
to propose this journey. It had, however,
become evident that his illness was increasing, and that the best medical treatment
could alone hold out a prospect of recovery.
The physicians at New Orleans had pronounced that, within a few months, he would
have to undergo an operation, and she could
not endure the thoughts of trusting to the
unskilful colonial surgeons. It seemed but
too probable that he would not henceforward be equal to the labours and fatigue of
a planter's existence; and the climate of
Louisiana was daily reducing his strength

and increasing his sufferings. She did not long hesitate, but with a cheerful smile proposed to him to sell the concessions, to part with St. Agathe! They had much increased in value during the last ten years, and their sale would realise a sum sufficient to insure them a small income. It was an effort and a sacrifice. St. Agathe was connected with the only happy period of her life. Her youth had revived in that beloved spot. There she had known the perfection of domestic happiness — there she had been blest as a wife and a mother, and almost worshipped by all about her. She had walked the earth with her head erect, her voice undisguised, and her heart at rest. No fears, no misgivings, had disturbed her sunny hours, or marred her nightly rest in its green shades and amidst its simple inhabitants. Since her arrival at New Orleans, sudden tremors had sometimes seized her at the sight of persons whose faces she fancied were familiar to her. Or, if a stranger's eyes followed her in the streets—and this often happened, for her beauty was more striking than it had been even in youth; her movements were so full of grace, and her figure so majestic, that it was difficult for her to pass unnoticed—she hurried on with a beating heart, or hastily drew down her veil. Old heart-aches had returned—thoughts of the past were oftener in her mind. She heard the news of her sister's death in a casual manner, and could not tell even Mina of her grief. Her residence in the French town was a foretaste of what would henceforward be her lot if St. Agathe was sold. It was deliberately closing the gates of her earthly paradise; but then she knew that what had been for ten years a paradise could be so no longer. Neither her husband nor herself could ever forget what they had gone through. There are associations which can never be cancelled. The people, the language, even the natural beauties of America, could not be to them what they once were. No; it was not a sacrifice she was making—on second thoughts she became conscious of this; but it was setting the seal to a doom which was already past recall.

The news from Europe was also preying more and more upon her mind. Two years had elapsed since notice of the Czar Peter's death had reached the colony; and now intelligence had just arrived of the Empress Catherine's decease. D'Auban had heard this one night at the governor's house, and had hastened home to tell his wife.

She anxiously asked, 'And what of my son?'

'He has been proclaimed emperor, and Mentzchikoff has taken charge of his person and of the reins of government.'

'Ah! I now understand why Catherine left him the crown, rather than to Anna Ivanovna. My poor child! in the hands of such men as Mentzchikoff and the Narishkins, what will become of him?'

'Was nothing more said?'

'No, that was all.'

'Madame d'Auban's lip quivered; and, gathering up her work, she hastened to a terrace which commanded a view of the sea —she felt a wish to be alone, to commune with herself on the news she had just heard; even her husband's presence was irksome at that moment. The forsaken child was uppermost in her mind; the change in his fate brought before her all kinds of new thoughts. He was now an emperor, a czar, that young boy whose face she so longed to see. She fancied the shouts of the people when he was proclaimed—the cries of 'Long live Peter the Second!' They seemed to ring in her ears as the waves broke gently on the shore; and then she wondered if he ever thought of his mother; if he ever noticed her picture; and whether that picture was hanging in the same place as it used to do, above the couch where she was sitting on the day when the baby of a year old had been brought to see her for the last time. Her name was on the frame, Charlotte of Brunswick Wolfenbuttel, born in 1796. Had they engraved on it the day of her death? 'He sees my picture,' she murmured; 'and when he goes to church, he sees my tomb. Does he ever see me in his dreams? I have sometimes dreamt of him very distinctly, and have awoke just as he was going to speak to me. Oh, my boy emperor, my young czar, my crowned child, would not you, perhaps, give half your empire to have a mother, on whose bosom you might lay your fair young head, in whose arms

you might find refuge from bad men and
secret foes? And why should we not meet
again? Why should there be an impassable
gulph between us, now that the czar is dead
and the empress also, and that my son, my
own son, reigns in their stead?' As these
thoughts passed through her mind, an ardent
desire to return to Europe took possession of
her; not that she formed any plan of regain-
ing her position; not that she did not shudder
at the thought of disclosing her existence,
and at the dangers and misery to her husband and herself which such a step might
involve in that old world, which, like M. de
Talleyrand, thought mistakes worse than
crimes, and *mésalliances* more degrading
than sin. She would have died sooner than
conceal her marriage; but secretly, perhaps,
she might venture to approach her son. If
the Countess de Konigsmark was still alive
—it was two years now since she had heard
from her—some communication might be
made to the young emperor, which would
re-establish her, not near his throne, indeed,
but as a living mother in his heart.

She spoke to her husband of their vague

thoughts and hopes, of the twofold reasons she now had to urge their return to France, and their decision was at last taken. D'Auban had doubted a long time; he had mistrusted his own intense longing to revisit his own country, and had felt afraid for his wife of a return to Europe; but an accidental circumstance which occurred at that time, but which he kept from her knowledge, hastened his acquiescence. He had never mentioned to her the orders which had been sent out from Europe, for the apprehension of persons suspected of the robbery of her own jewels. The reports which had been circulated regarding M. de Chambelle and herself had apparently died away since his death and her marriage, but he had never felt perfectly easy on the subject, and about this time he met in the streets Reinhart, the very man who had been most active in spreading them. The next day he saw him hovering near his house, as if watching its inmates. This circumstance determined him to leave the colony. A purchaser was found for the United Concessions, and St. Agathe was sold. They agreed to transmit to Paris the sum thus realised, and to proceed to France by the next vessel which should sail from New Orleans. Their intention was to spend there the time necessary for the treatment of his malady, and, when his health was re-established, to seek for a post under government in some of the dependencies of France. The services he had rendered during the insurrection entitled him, he thought, to such an appointment; and he had friends who, he hoped, would lend him their assistance in advancing his claims. She nursed besides many a romantic vision, many a dream of a journey to Russia and a secret interview with her son; but these were silently indulged and cherished, not even her husband knew how much she built upon them.

It was with more than childish grief that Mina fixed her eyes on the coasts of America, as the 'Ville de Paris' heaved her anchor, and the wind from the shore wafted the perfume of the orange flower from the gardens of the French colonists. Her mother sighed as she saw the tears which filled her eyes, and sorrowfully asked herself if her daughter was destined to be always, like herself, a wanderer on the face of the earth.

'A year, mamma, is not that what you said?' whispered Mina, trying to smile. 'A year, and then we shall return to St. Agathe?'

Madame d'Auban stroked her cheek without answering. She wished to keep from her the knowledge of the sale of St. Agathe, till the sight of other countries and the awakening of other interests had diminished the vividness of her recollections.

'Papa will be quite well in a year, and then we can go back; and what joy there will be in the Mission when we arrive! They will all come out to meet us with garlands and with songs, as they used to do when dear Father Maret and the hunters returned from the forests. We shall be so happy!'

She was hoping against hope, poor child. There was in her mind a suspicion of the truth, and she spoke in this way in order to be reassured. When she saw her mother did not answer, she slipped away and sat down alone in another part of the vessel. Her father went to look for her; she threw herself into his arms, hid her face in his breast, and wept—

Like a slight young tree, that throws
The weight of rain from its drooping boughs.

But when she raised her head again,

The cloud on her soul that lay,
Had melted in glittering drops away.

She had conquered her grief and gladdened
his heart with one of her radiant smiles.
The spirit which had made her, from a baby,
a ruler among her companions, had been,
during the last two years, trained and turned
in another direction. The trials of her school-
life had taught her to rule herself.

The arrival at a place we have not seen
for many years, the sight of objects familiar
to us in our youth—of things we recollect,
and of others which have changed the aspect
of the picture imprinted in our memory, has
generally something melancholy in it—sometimes only a pleasing sadness, sometimes a
heavy gloom. When it is a quiet country
landscape we gaze on, or a fine extensive
view of sea and land, or a mountainous re-
gion half-way between us and the sky—such
reminiscences are far less depressing than
when they are connected with the busy

haunts of men, the great thoroughfares of life. In a great city, when you enter an hotel and have nothing to do but to sit down and think, when every sight and sound is at once familiar and strange, when for many a long hour you are alone in the midst of an ever-rolling tide of human beings, the feeling of solitude is painfully oppressive : there is not a book on your table ; no one knocks at your door ; the postman brings you no letter ; carriages roll in the street, but they do no stop ; you mechanically listen to the increasing and decreasing noise as they approach, go by, and recede ; you go to the window and watch the passengers, all intent upon something, and feel as if you, alone in the world, had nothing to do, and were stranded for the time being on the shore of the great stream of human life.

M. and Madame d'Auban experienced this very powerfully on the day when they took up their residence in a small lodging which a friend had engaged for them in one of the old-fashioned streets of the Faubourg St. Germain. To be once more in Paris, and to be there together, seemed so extraordinary. The commonplace aspect of everything about them was in itself singular. D'Auban was very tired with the long journey, and so was Mina. He sat down near the window and fell into a fit of musing. Mina placed herself on a stool at his feet and watched with a frowning countenance the carriages and foot-passengers; then she took out her pocket-book and wrote in it the following remarks : 'August 5th, 1730. We are just arrived at Paris. It is a very ugly, melancholy place—not at all like the Illinois or Louisiana ; it is like a great forest of houses. Men have made this forest, and Almighty God the great forests of the new world ; I like best Almighty God's work. Papa and mamma do not look happy; and I do not like France. · I do not agree with Mary Queen of Scots, who said, " Adieu, plaisant pays de France." I say, with a deep sigh, " Bonjour, triste pays de France." She had never seen the new beautiful France where I was born—where I used to lie down on the grass under the pine-groves, watching the sunshine through the green branches—where every one was kind to us. I want to go back.'

The pencil dropped from the young

girl's hand, and her head rested against her father's knee. She had fallen asleep. He picked up the pocket-book and read what she had written. A rather sad smile crossed his lips; then taking his daughter in his arms, he carried her into the back room and laid her on the bed without awaking her.

Madame d'Auban, meanwhile, was taking off her travelling dress and unpacking her things. Once, in passing before a looking-glass, she stopped and looked attentively at her own face. It was still a very beautiful one, and the expression of her matchless eyes was as lovely as ever—but of that she could not judge. It struck her that she looked much older, and that no one who had known her in former days would be the least likely to recognise her. 'How foolish I am,' she thought, 'to be always so afraid of seeing people! I will try to feel and to do like others; to shake off my nervousness, and make acquaintance with my husband's friends. If they ask me what my maiden name was, what shall I say?' She smiled to herself, and said, half aloud, 'Mdlle. Désillinois.'

When she went into the sitting-room, her husband raised his head languidly and said—
' I wonder, after all, why we came here.'

She looked at him anxiously, and sitting down by his side, answered, ' Because I would come ; because I care more for your health than for anything else on earth. O my own! my own!' she exclaimed with passionate tenderness ; ' my beloved one ! friend to more than human friendship true ! what, without you, would life be to me?'

' No, no,' d'Auban replied with a troubled look, and speaking in an agitated manner. ' I ought not to have married you. I should have insisted on restoring you to your kindred.'

' How can you speak in that way ? it was impossible,' said his wife, half impatiently.

' Oh, I don't know. Selfish passion often deceives us, and happiness hardens the heart. During all our years of bliss it never occurred to me that I had dealt unjustly by you ; but since I have been ill, and have seen you wearing yourself out in nursing me, and since the horrible dangers you ran two years ago, a terrible self-reproach pur-

sues me ; it is that, as much as the climate,
that has made me ill. . . .'

'And you let this go on without telling
me that you had such a wrong, such a
foolish thought! O Henri, I can hardly
forgive you. . . .'

'What was the use of speaking? Have
I not bound you to me by irrevocable
ties? Have I not irreparably injured you?
No, when everything about you was bright
and beautiful, and I could spend every hour
in working and in planning for your happiness; when every one who came near you
loved you and was kind—as that dear child
wrote in her journal a moment ago—it did
not appear to me in that light. I did not
regret for you the loss of a position which, but
for me, you might yet regain. But here, in
this mean lodging, where no one notices
your arrival or gives you a welcome; you,
who would once have been lodged in a
palace and had princes and nobles at your
feet; here, where I foresee what you may
have to suffer with and for me . . . . Oh,
my dear heart, it is more than I can
endure. . . .'

His wife laid her hand on his, and there
was a tone of indignant tenderness in her
voice as she replied, 'Henri, banish, crush
such thoughts as you would an unworthy
temptation! They pain, they wrong me.
What next to faith in Him is God's best gift
to a woman? Is it not the love of a noble
heart? To you I owe every joy I have
known on earth, and under Him every hope
of heaven. You have taught, consoled, in-
structed, and guided me. You saved my life,
alas! at what a cost He knows, and so do
I. What robbed you of your strength?
what ruined your health? How can you
talk to me of my kindred, of palaces and
princes? Henri, are you not the light of my
eyes, the beloved of my heart, dearer and
better to me than ten sons? O God, forgive
me!' she passionately exclaimed, falling on
her knees; 'forgive me if I have loved one
of Thy creatures too much—if in my happiness I have not thought enough of my poor
boy. If even now poverty, suffering with
my husband is joy compared to the brightest
fate on earth without him. O Henri!' she said,
turning to him again, 'you must have little

known of my love to speak as you did
just now. Never again say you have wronged
me ; I cannot bear it.'

D'Auban was deeply moved, and seized her
hand. 'Forgive me, my love, forgive me,'
he cried. 'I did not mean thus to agitate
you ; but the wild thought did pass through
my mind before you spoke that even now I
ought to run the risk of being parted from
you—that I ought to make your name and
position known, and to relinquish the offer ;
yes, I thought it might be my duty, a blessing
I do not deserve.'

'What words are these, Henri? what evil
spirit has whispered this accursed thought
in my husband's ear? It did not reach your
heart—by my own I know it did not. O hated
France ! detested Europe ! poisonous air of an
old corrupted world ! Sooner had we both died
by the hands of the Natches, sooner perished
on the shores where we first met and first loved,
than that you should deem it possible we should
part. Listen to me, Henri. If in the first days
of our happiness, when there was not a grey
hair on your head, when your arm was so
strong that you could carry me like an infant

over the streams of St. Agathe, I should have refused to separate from you even for the sake of my son, or for any other affection or interest in the world, do you think I would do so now, when your strength has been spent for me, and that during twelve blessed years I have learnt every day to love you more ? Do you not remember that that God, the God whom you have taught me to know and serve, has said that those whom He has joined together men may never sunder ? But we have been talking like two foolish creatures—you to frighten me so uselessly, and I to take it to heart and answer you seriously.'

'Well,' said d'Auban, with a half-sad, half-pleased smile, 'I believe it was a fit of insanity ; and yet——'

'A good night's rest will restore your senses, dearest heart ; and to-morrow you must go and see your friends the d'Orgevilles, and prepare to introduce to them your wife ; and we must find out who is the best physician we can consult, and then begin to see a little of this wonderful city. Mina, and I too indeed, will stare at every-

thing like savages. I must also learn a little
French housekeeping. Our hostess will put
me in the way of it. She has promised to
show us the way to St. Sulpice to-morrow
morning. You must lie in bed and rest.
But when once Mina has been into a church,
she will feel at home in Paris, and not consider it quite such an uncouth place as she
does to-day.'

D'Auban smiled more gaily, and during
the rest of the evening watched her light
and graceful movements as she passed from
one room to the other, unpacking their
clothes and books, and gradually giving a
more cheerful look to the dingy little apartment. He thought she looked so like a
princess, that it seemed to him difficult the
world should not recognise the imprint of
royalty on her fair brow and graceful form.

The next day he went to the Hôtel d'Orgeville, and was shown into the same salon
where, so many years ago, he had spent hour
after hour. Scarcely an article of furniture
had been moved from the place in which he
remembered it. The red velvet sofas and
high-backed chairs, and the fauteuil where

the mistress of the house used to sit when she received company of an evening; the antique cabinets with folding doors, and the étagères loaded with china; the portraits on the walls—everything was looking just as it did on the night when he had conversed about emigration with M. de Mesme and M. Maret, and for the first time thought seriously of going to America.

When Madame d'Orgeville came into the room, he perceived that her face, if not her furniture, bore witness to the lapse of years. Her hair had turned white, and rouge supplied the place of her former bloom. Nothing could be more cordial than her greeting:

'Ah! my dear colonel,' she exclaimed, seizing both his hands, 'how charmed I am to see you! What centuries it is since we have met! and how many things have happened! But you are not looking well?'

'I am very far from well,' he answered. 'We colonists go in search of fortune, madame, and often lose health, the greater blessing of the two.'

'And have you made your fortune?'

'Not anything to boast of—a livelihood, my dear friend, nothing more. The Natches' insurrection depreciated the value of property in New France at the time I was obliged to sell. As soon as I get well, I intend to try and obtain employment in the colonies— if possible in the Antilles.'

'You do not mean, then, to return to Louisiana?'

'No, madame, not if I can help it.'

'I am not surprised at that, after all you went through, and the terrible scenes you witnessed, your wife and your child so nearly perishing, and your arriving only just in time to rescue them and the other captives. I assure you it was much spoken of at the time, and you are considered quite a hero. So many people will be wanting to see you, I expect you will be quite the fashion. M. Maret showed us the interesting account you wrote to him of his brother's death. By the way, you will meet him if you come here this evening. He may be of use to you about the appointment you want. He is in high favour at present with monsieur le prince.'

D'Auban could scarcely refrain from smiling—it was so exactly the same thing over again, as in past years. Before he had time to answer, Madame d'Orgeville went on:

'And now tell me about your marriage. Madame d'Auban is French, I suppose?'

'Her mother was a German. Her father's name was M. de Chambelle. I suppose you never heard of the family; but I assure you that she is une demoiselle de très-bonne maison.'

'And a good parti, I hope.'

'She brought me, as her dower, a concession of some importance, which, had my health allowed me to remain in America, might have proved valuable; but we sold everything before leaving America.'

'And you have a daughter?'

'Yes, a little creole of twelve years old, who looks at least fifteen. I hope you will let me introduce her to you.'

'Most willingly. And now that I think of it, my carriage is at the door. Allow me to reconduct you to your home, and then I may have, perhaps, at once the pleasure of making Madame d'Auban's acquaintance.'

D'Auban assented, for he thought that the sooner his wife got over the nervousness she felt at the sight of strangers the better it would be, and his intimate friends she must needs see during her stay in Paris. Madame d'Orgeville wished to show her old friend every kindness, but she was also very curious to see his wife. Some of her acquaintances, who had been at New Orleans, had spoken in terms of admiration of her grace and beauty; but she did not trust to their taste, and was anxious to judge for herself before inviting her to her house.

She was taken by surprise, not so much by Madame d'Auban's beauty, as by the singular distinction of her manner, and the pure and refined French which she spoke. With the freedom of Parisian manners, and the privilege which people who are at the head of a coterie sometimes assume of saying whatever comes into their head, she exclaimed, in the midst of her conversation with her, 'Good heavens! how handsome you are, madame, and what perfect French you speak! Quite the language of the Court, with only a shade of German accent. And

your manners, your voice, your whole appearance! I assure you I should have
thought you had always lived in Paris.'

Madame d'Auban smiled; but Mina, who
was being led into the room at that moment
by her father, heard Madame d'Orgeville's
words, and deeply resented them. 'Why
should not mamma be beautiful,' she thought,
'and why should she not be perfect in every
way, though she has not lived in this odious
Paris?' Mina's face was one of those which
a frown becomes almost as much as a smile,
and when, after kissing her on both cheeks,
Madame d'Orgeville called her a charming
creole, the indignant look which she put on
made her look so pretty, that that lady,
during the rest of her visit, could hardly
take her eyes off her. 'She is quite as pretty
as Madame de Prie,' she thought, 'and with
an expression of purity and innocence such
as I have never yet seen. That face will
make her fortune, if it does not prove her
ruin. I am rather glad my daughters are
not so strikingly beautiful. I believe the
safest thing for a woman is to be tolerably
good-looking, and have a good dowery.'

Whilst these reflections were passing through her mind she was, with that wonderful power some people possess of being engrossed with two subjects at once, most earnestly recommending to Madame d'Auban a physician of the name of Lenoir, who, she assured her, was one of the first medical men in Paris. She ended by inviting them all to dinner for the next day, and proposed that Mina should spend the afternoon with her daughters and some of their friends.

That afternoon proved a beautiful one. The weather was warm without being hot, the sun shining brightly, and the sky cloudless. The garden of the Hôtel d'Orgeville was full of autumnal flowers, choice roses and China asters. The trees were beginning to put on their brown and red colouring, and the grass plot in the centre was studded with buttercups and daisies.

Mina, who for months had not seen a garden, and scarcely a flower, was in ecstasies. The wearisome sea voyage had been succeeded by the journey to Paris in a close diligence, and two days in the *entresol* of the Rue des Saints Pères. If she had been alone, her delight would have been unbounded. As it was, she could not resist taking a run across the grass, and timidly asking Julie d'Orgeville if she might gather some buttercups—a permission which was graciously granted, with a rather supercilious smile, for Mdlle. d'Auban was half a head taller than Mdlle. Julie, and for a girl of that height she deemed it rather a childish amusement. The young ladies sat down on a semicircular stone bench at the end of an alley of plane-trees, and began to converse in an undertone, which gradually rose to a higher key, as the subjects under discussion became more interesting. A little girl of ten years of age asked what they were going to play at.

Mademoiselle d'Orgeville said, 'We most of us prefer conversation; but you may, if you like, propose to the younger part of the society to play at ladies.'

'What will she do?' said the leader of the younger ones, pointing to Mina.

'What would you like best, Mdlle. d'Auban?' asked Julie, with great civility.

'What do you do when you play at

ladies?' inquired the latter, raising her large blue eyes from the flowers she had on her knees.

'Oh, one is Madame la Duchesse, and another Madame la Princesse, and another Madame la Marquise, and so on.'

'Then one, you know, has *les grandes entrées* at Court,' cried a little girl.

'And the duchesses have tabourets,' said another.

'And then we stand at the door of the arbour, and pretend it is the queen's dressing-room; and we go in according to our ranks and stand by her Majesty; and Madame la Duchesse hands her her shift, if there is no one of higher rank in the room; but if one of the princesses comes in, she, of course, gives it up to her. . . . '

'Which is to be the queen?' asked Mina, looking round the circle.

'We always draw lots for that. By the way, do you know, mesdemoiselles, that my mother says that yesterday, at the funeral of the Princesse de Conti, Madame la Duchesse de Boufflers pushed by, and would not let Mademoiselle de Clermont sprinkle

the corpse before she had done so herself.
But she had all the trouble in the world to
prevent it.'

'But my papa says that it is quite ridicu-
lous to suppose that duchesses have that
right.'

'Then your papa is mistaken, mademoiselle. And if I play at going to Court to-day,
I shall be Madame de Boufflers, and nothing
shall induce me to yield up that point.'

'Well, all I know is that I went to see
Mdlle. de St. Simon yesterday, and that she
says the pretensions of the Duchesse de
Boufflers are quite shocking, and that she
should never have taken precedency of
Mademoiselle de Clermont, who was repre-
senting the Queen.'

'Who cares what that ugly girl says? She
is like a note of interrogation—a little crooked
thing, always asking questions, or laying
down the law like the cross old duke her
father.'

'Would you like to be the queen, Mademoiselle d'Auban? You may if you like,'
said the leader of the youthful band.

'No, thank you,' answered Mina; 'I should

not know how to behave.' She thought of her grassy throne, and her sable courtiers who used to call her their chief, in the green prairies far away; but that was not like playing at being the queen of France, and she said she should like better to stay where she was, and to tie up her buttercups.

An animated conversation was carried on by the elder girls, which chiefly related to their various prospects, and the intentions of their parents with regard to their establishment in life. Some were already engaged to be married, though they had never seen their future husbands. Some were to be married as soon as a suitable alliance could be found for them. Some hoped, and some feared, they might have to go into religion. They talked of the good luck of one of their friends, who had become the wife of a gentleman whose position at Court would enable her to take precedency of her sister, who had wedded, the year before, a wealthy jurisconsulte, a cousin of the Messieurs Paris. One young lady they mentioned, Alice le Pelletier, was actually about to be married to the son of a duc et pair. ' But then, you

know, she is immensely rich,' said Julie
d'Orgeville, ' and her mother was a Beaufort.
Do your parents intend to marry you in
France, Mademoiselle d'Auban?' she asked
of Mina, who answered with simplicity—

' I don't think they mean to marry me
at all.'

' Are you, then, going into religion ? '

' I have never thought of it,' Mina said.

' I suppose you have thought of very little
yet, my dear, but playthings and sweetmeats,' said Julie, good-humouredly, but in
rather a contemptuous manner.

Mina blushed, but made no reply. How
little the elder girl knew of the depths of
thought and feeling in the soul of that child,
who had gone through more emotions, and
waged more inward battles, and exercised
more virtues already, than she had ever
dreamt of in her limited sphere of thought
and action! Julie d'Orgeville was not without amiable qualities, and her principles
were good; so were those of many of the
young girls gathered together on that occasion. Some of them eventually became
excellent wives and mothers, and exemplary

fervent nuns. But they were impregnated for the time with the levity and the prejudices of the worldly society to which they belonged, and reflected in a childish form the aspect it presented.

Mina felt miserably at a loss in their company. They were neither like women nor like children. She could not reach high enough, or descend low enough, to be on a level with them; hers had been such a totally different training. Crime and virtue, innocence and guilt, are perhaps less strange to each other, as far as sympathy goes, than worldliness and unworldliness. Erring souls sometimes appreciate goodness. Where there is guilt there is often remorse, and remorse is feeling. But the worshippers of rank, fashion, and wealth look with a comfortable sense of superiority on those who do not adore the same idols as themselves. A worldly child sounds like a singular anomaly, but the thing exists, and the principles of worldliness are never so broadly displayed as in such cases; for childhood is consistent; thoughts, words, and actions are all in accordance. Plausibility is the growth of a more

advanced period of life; a slowly-acquired
quality which it requires time to mature.

Mina's parents felt in some ways as little
at home in the salon of the Hôtel d'Orgeville
as she did in the schoolroom.   After so long
an absence they were not conversant with
the state of parties such as it existed at that
time in Paris, or with the intrigues which
were carried on in the court and in the
town.   The tone of society often astonished
them.   People who were reckoned good said
very strange things in those days, and allowed
themselves an extraordinary latitude of
thought and speech.   D'Auban had left Paris
at the end of the reign of Louis XIV.   The
whole period of the Regency had gone by
during his absence, and impressed on French
society dire traces of its influence.   His wife
had witnessed in Russia crime and brutality,
degrading vices and coarse buffoonery, but
the polished iniquity, the ruthless levity of
Parisian manners was new to her.   They
were also no doubt changed themselves by the
solitary earnest lives they had led, by the holy
joys and sacred sorrows they had experienced,
and felt more deeply than others would have

done the pain of witnessing the increasing immorality and irreligion of the higher classes of French society; of hearing the praises of vile miscreants and poisonous writings from the lips of men who still believed in Christianity, who went through the forms of religion, and summoned priests to their deathbeds; of watching the rising tide of corruption which was to widen and deepen for fifty years till the foundations of the throne and the altar fell to the ground, and the deluge of the revolution swept away every landmark. The epoch in question was indeed the beginning of that terrible end, and more trying perhaps to the true of heart than the fatal consummation which, with all its horrors and its sufferings, gave evidence of the faith and goodness latent in many of those who had sported on the brink of the precipice, but when it opened under their feet became martyrs or heroes.

The 18th century is a sad picture to look back upon, but in the midst of all its sin and growing unbelief what redeeming instances of virtue and purity mark the pages of its history! Where can more admirable models be found of true and undefiled religion than in the wife, the son, and the daughter of Louis XV.? In the same palace, under the same roof as Madame de Pompadour, Marie Leckzinska, the Dauphin, his Saxon wife, and Mesdames de France served God and loved the poor with a humble fidelity and patient perseverance which surprise us when we read their biographies and remember the age and the Court in which their lot was cast.

At the time when Madame d'Auban was in Paris, the young king of France was still devoted to his wife. With an open brow and a bright smile he would say, when another woman's beauty was insidiously commended in his presence, 'She is not, I am certain, as handsome as the queen.' So he thought and felt as long as the wickedness of his courtiers and their vile instruments had not seduced him from his allegiance to his gentle wife. But they laid their plans with consummate skill. They carried them on with diabolical art; they took advantage of his weakness; step by step they dragged him down into the abyss of degradation in which his latter years were sunk. They turned the idol of his people, the well-beloved of a great nation, into the abject slave of Madame Dubarry, the mark of a withering scorn, the disgrace of a polluted throne.

Is there a greater sin, one that cries more loudly to heaven for vengeance, than the cold-blooded, deliberate design of ruining the happiness and poisoning the peace of those whose own souls are not only at stake, but whose example may influence thousands for good or for evil? Who can foresee the consequences of such guilt, if successful? Who can say that the crimes of the French Revolution, the murder of an innocent king, the more than murder of his consort and his sister, the tortures of his hapless child, will not be laid on the Day of Judgment at the door of those who conspired to ruin the domestic happiness of Louis XV., and to drag him down to the level of their own ignominy? God forgive them; though we can scarcely add, 'They knew not what they did!'

Thoughts akin to these were in Madame d'Auban's mind, and made her woman's heart throb with indignation when she heard one day in Madame d'Orgeville's salon, a group of men and women of the world turning into ridicule the king's affection for the queen, and predicting, with exultation, that, thanks to the manœuvres of the Ducs d'Epernon and de Gesore, and the dawning charms of Madame de Mailly, it would not be of long duration. She had known the pangs of desertion, the anguish which hides itself under forced smiles, the utter helplessness of an injured wife, more helpless on or near a throne than in a cottage, because her sufferings are watched and her tears counted.

'Poor queen,' she inwardly exclaimed, 'poor Marie Leckzinska! If a man stabbed thee to the heart he would be broken on a wheel; but how many assassins there are who are not punished in this world!' Monsieur Maret was sitting by her at that moment; she said a word or two which showed on what subject her thoughts were running. 'But would it have been possible to expect,' he answered, 'that the queen should go through life without some great sufferings? Is there not always some striking compensation to be looked for in the destiny

of a person who has been singularly favoured
by fortune ?   Picture to yourself, if you can,
madame, a more unexampled instance of
good luck than hers.'

'It remains to be seen,' said Madame
d'Auban, ' if, after all, her unforeseen elevation to the throne proves so great a blessing.
But explain to me, sir, how it happened that
the penniless daughter of a dethroned sovereign should have become the bride of Louis
XV.'

'The Duc de Bourbon, or rather Madame
de Prie, who rules in his name, considered
that the future queen might prove a dangerous element of opposition to his ministry
if he did not secure her allegiance to him by
the tie of gratitude.   And so they bethought
themselves of the daughter of King Stanislaus,
whom the regent had permited out of charity
to inhabit an old mansion half in ruins in
Weissenburg. Conceive the moment when
this poor king opened the Duc de Bourbon's
letter, perhaps fearing an order to leave France
within twenty-four hours, and then found it
contained a proposal of marriage from the King
of France to his daughter !   From the King

of France! who had just sent back an in-
fanta, and for the sake of whose alliance
every monarch in Europe would have given
one of his fairest provinces. I wonder he
did not die of joy!'

'I wonder what *she* felt,' ejaculated
Madame d'Auban, who was thinking of the
day when her own father had said to her,
'My daughter, I wish you joy. The Czar Peter
has chosen you from amongst thirteen German princesses to be the Czarovitch's bride.'

'The Duc d'Antin has told us that
Stanislaus went straight into the room
where his wife and daughter were mending
their linen, and said, "Let us kneel down and
thank God." "O dear father!" the princess
exclaimed, "are you restored to the throne
of Poland?" "No, my daughter; it is something better than that. You are Queen of
France." She had just been refused by the
Duke of Baden! D'Auban went to Stras-
burg with the Duc de Beauvilliers to compliment the bride. He had to make a speech
and he committed a comical blunder, an
egregious one for such a courtier! In his
address to the Princess he said that M. le

Duc might have chosen a Queen of France amongst his own sisters, but virtue was what he was seeking for, and he knew where to look for it.'

Mdlle. de Clermont, who is mistress of the Princess's household, was standing behind her chair, and whispered to the person next to her, 'What does M. d'Antin take us for, my sisters and myself?'

Madame d'Auban smiled, and was going to make some observation in reply, when the door was thrown open and his Excellency the Russian Ambassador was announced.

D'Auban had ascertained that the persons composing the Russian Embassy at Paris had none of them been at St. Petersburgh at the time when they could have seen his wife. Still he looked towards her with uneasiness when Prince Kourakin came in. He saw her colour at the first moment, and then turn very pale. There were not many persons in the room. When the ambassador had paid his compliments to the mistress of the house, the conversation became general.

M. d'Orgeville asked if there was any news.

'Great news from my court,' said Prince
Kourakin. 'I have just received despatches
containing the anouncement of a *coup d'état*
at St. Petersburgh.'

'What! what!' exclaimed several persons,
amongst whom was d'Auban, who saw his
wife's eyes   ed upon Prince Kourakin with
intense anxiety.

'Mentzchikoff is overthrown and on his
way to Siberia!'

'Incredible! wonderful!' cried Madame
d'Orgeville.   'What an important event!
Whose doing is it?

'Our Imperial Master's.   Mentzchikoff
had, as you know, betrothed him to his own
daughter and kept him in a state of absolute
subjection.   The Czar could not walk, or
ride, or eat, or speak but by the orders of
his minister.   This was carried on a little
too far and a little too long.   It is not safe
to bully a lion's whelp.   You cannot foresee
the moment when he will find out he is a
lion.'

'And he has done so now?' said M.
Maret.

'With a vengeance; he has roared to some
effect, too.'

'I am delighted to hear it,' cried Madame d'Orgeville. 'You must forgive me, my dear ambassador, but I could never get over the pastry-cook's elevation; the cakes stuck in my throat.'

Kourakin shrugged his shoulders and took snuff. 'I might say the same if the poor man was not now in disgrace. One does not like to speak ill of the fallen.'

'Then, why did he not say so when the poor man was on his legs?' whispered M. Maret to Madame d'Auban, who did not hear him, and was breathlessly watching for Kourakin's next words, and trembling lest the subject should drop. But everybody wished to hear the details of the minister's fall, and he said, 'You remember Dolgorouki?' He was here with the Czar Peter some years ago. His son and the little Princess Elizabeth were the czar's only playfellows. Young Dolgorouki always slept in his room, and took every occasion to excite his young sovereign's resentment against Mentzchikoff. On the 5th of last month he was staying with him at Peterhoff. There he received orders from his father to persuade the czar

to jump out of window in the night, and
make his way to a spot where an escort was
to be in readiness to conduct him to St.
Petersburgh ; everything was prepared in the
city for an outbreak against the minister.
The young monarch was nothing loth, and
reached the capital in safety.   Once there
the imperial guard, the army, and the people,
excited by the Dolgoroukis, gathered round
the prince, with loud cries of ' Long live the
Czar ! ' ' Long live Peter the Second ! ' 'Down
with Mentzchikoff !' and by the time the minister heard of the plot, his cause was hopeless, and his banishment decreed.   By this
time he must be moralising at Yakouska,
unless he has died on the way of grief and
spite.   It is supposed the czar will marry
the sister of young Dolgorouki.

' This is a most interesting episode,' observed one lady.   ' And I know nothing to
be compared to it in suddenness, since poor
M. Fouquet's disgrace.'

' M. de Fréjus narrowly escaped a similar
fate,' said M. Maret.

' Ah ! the wily churchman,' cried Kourakin,
' took quite a different line with his royal
royal pupil than ' . . .

'The pastry-cook with his,' interrupted Madame d'Orgeville; 'and it has certainly answered better.'

'For my part,' said the Russian ambassador, a little nettled, 'I like better to see a young monarch dismiss an arrogant minister, than cry over the loss of a favourite tutor like a child after its nurse.'

A few more remarks were made, and then the conversation turned to other topics. When M. d'Auban, his wife, and his little girl returned home that night, they all looked ill and tired. Madame d'Auban could not sleep that night, or if she closed her eyes a moment, her dreams were agitating. Waking and sleeping she kept revisiting the land where her son was reigning, and picturing to herself what had recently taken place in those scenes she knew so well: at Peterhoff, the imperial boy leaping out of the window in the darkness of the night; in St. Petersburgh, the people hailing him like a rescued captive. She felt proud of the energy he had shown. She was glad he had escaped from an unworthy thraldom, but how would he use his liberty, and how wield the

fatal sceptre of irresponsible power? Haunted
by visions of tortured criminals, of bar-
barous executions and degrading buffooneries,
she shuddered at the thought of her son in
the midst of such a court, and growing familiar with vice and cruelty, till her mother's
heart could scarcely endure the anguish.
She rose from her sleepless bed to pray that
she might soon force her way to his side,
and speak to him, if it was only once,
of justice and of mercy, of God and of
eternity. During those hours of the night
when one idea engrosses the mind with all-
absorbing power, it seemed to her as if she
must set out for Russia the very next day.
Wild projects of revealing her existence to
the King of France or Prince Kourakin
flitted through her brain, but they vanished
with the morning light. She had already
ascertained that the Countess de Konigsmark
had died a short time ago, after a lingering
illness of nearly two years, which latter circumstance accounted for her silence since the
death of the Czar Peter. Of the two other
persons who had been concerned in the plot

for her escape, she had no means of hearing. Their obscure situation made it more difficult to ascertain what had become of them. But her anxiety on this point was superseded, and all idea of leaving Paris put an end to for a time, by her husband's increasing illness.

For many succeeding weeks she had but one thought and one care. Dr. Lenoir was called in. He proved to be a relative of Madame d'Auban's fellow-captive in Louisiana, and had heard of her kindness to the poor foolish creature, as he disrespectfully called his brother's widow. Colonel d'Auban's case, he said, required profound repose of body and mind. His strength was to be sustained by every possible means, and everything agitating or painful as far as possible kept from him. Under favourable circumstances he would venture to predict a complete recovery, otherwise he would not be answerable for his life. This was the opinion he privately gave to Madame d'Auban. The treatment would probably last about four months—good air and a cheerful situation,

within reach of his own daily visits, he
deemed indispensable.

When he had left the room, Madame
d'Auban collected her thoughts and made
her calculations. There would not be, at
present, any question of their going into
society ; and this she was glad of, except for
one reason—she might lose the chance of
hearing news from Russia ; but still she hoped
that this loss might be supplied by the visits
at home of a few intimate friends. Mina
should continue to go to the Hôtel d'Orgeville, in order to acquire, in the society of
the young people she met there, the manners of her own country. The next thing
to be considered was the removal to another house; and now came the question of
means. This was the first time in her life
that she had had to face that vulgar difficulty. Her own and her husband's money
had been embarked in their concessions.
The forced sale of their property had been
disadvantageous ; and the capital they remained possessed of supplied a very limited
income. On the other hand, airy and
comfortable apartments in Paris were ex-

pensive, and so would be Dr. Lenoir's attendance.

For the first time, Madame d'Auban felt to care for riches. For the first time she became acquainted with the sting of poverty. She looked at her husband, remembered the physician's words, and mentally resolved that, with God's blessing, no care, no anxiety, should impede his recovery—that she alone would bear the burden of solicitude. In a playful manner, with gentleness and tact, she told him what the doctor had said, and demanded, in a smiling but urgent manner, the entire control and management of their expenses.

'My dear heart,' he said, fondly kissing her hand, ' what do you know of business? How can you manage the affairs of a poor gentilhomme ? '

'Better, perhaps, than you imagine, M. d'Auban. Nay, for once,' she said, with a graceful dignity which became her well, 'I will assert a woman's, a princess's, right to have her own way. Leave everything to me, dearest Henri. I will it as a wife: I claim it, too.'

'By your divine right to rule over the heart and will of your husband, I suppose. But, my beloved one, I cannot suffer that dear head, which ought to have worn a crown, to ache over accounts.'

She laid her finger on his lips, and, by loving words and caresses, put an end to his remonstrances.

Two days afterwards a cheerful, pretty apartment in the quartier du Louvre was engaged; the invalid's couch, placed near a window commanding a view of the Seine, the Isle de Paris, and the old towers of Notre Dame. Books lent by various friends were laid on the table near him; and every morning Mina brought in bright-coloured flowers to make the room look gay. She bought them at the Marché aux Fleurs, as she walked home from an early mass. M. Lenoir came every day; his conversation entertained his patient, whilst his remedies improved his health. Old friends now and then called of an evening; and all who came into that little sanctuary of peace and love were charmed with Madame d'Auban. A good-natured curiosity was felt about her.

Every one wondered that so refined and
agreeable a person had been met with in a
remote colony. Full of intelligence, and of
the best sort of cleverness for a woman—
that of appreciating the talents and wit of
others—she knew how to promote conversation, without joining very much in it herself.
Her very speaking eyes answered, ques-
tioned, applauded, or remonstrated; and gave
continual evidence of her interest in what
others were saying. People were often
astonished to find that a person who spoke
so little could be such a pleasant member of
society. They little knew how hard it was
at times to keep the appearance of cheerful-
ness—how anxiously she was listening for
any word which might refer to Russia!
seldom daring to ask a direct question, and
never looking into a newspaper without a
beating heart.

She would sometimes mention her son to
her husband, in a casual manner and without
any appearance of emotion, that he might
not think she was pining for the moment
when he could accompany her to St. Petersburgh—a scheme long cherished—and which

she was more bent upon than ever, since
she had heard of the young monarch's
emancipation. It seemed to her as if she
now might find means of approaching him
—of telling him, and no one else, the secret
of her life—of whispering words of counsel
and warning, even as if a departed mother
had risen from her grave to haunt him with
her love. Dreams they were, wild hopeless
dreams, perhaps, but to her they did not
seem so. And the while she had made the
sacrifice of the only means she had of per-
forming this journey. The only valuable
possession she had retained was the locket,
with the czar's picture set in diamonds;
those diamonds she had always intended to
sell for this purpose, but she had parted with
them now. The sum thus obtained had
been partly employed in meeting the expenses of her husband's illness, and the rest
she retained for any future emergency of
the same kind. When he had asked her
how she was able to manage so well with
such limited resources, she had answered
that she had disposed of trifles she had no use

for. It never occurred to him that she had parted with those diamonds.

Now and then news accidently reached her of the land where her son reigned. Since the death of the Countess of Konigsmark she had no chance of direct information; but some one said one day that the Empress Eudoxia had been recalled to court by her grandson; and another time she read in the 'Mercure de France' that the Princess Mentzchikoff had died of a broken heart, on her way to Siberia; she sighed, for this poor woman had been kind to her once. And when she heard of her son's approaching nuptials with the Princess Dolgorouki, she breathed a fervent prayer that his marriage might be more blest than hers with his father. And the days went by, apparently like one another, though so full to her of hope, fear, and agitations, and at last there came one which had a great influence over her future fate.

CHAPTER V.

Qui survient ? Dame belle et fière
Son carrosse au galop conduit,
Jette à l'autre un flot de poussière
Et l'accrochant fait rire et fuit.
Béranger.

For I saw her as I thought dead,
And have in vain said
Many a prayer upon her grave.
Shakspeare.

SOME months after their change of abode, in the
afternoon of a day warm as early spring days
are wont to be in Paris, Madame d'Auban
was walking with her daughter in the
Tuileries gardens.   The horse-chestnut trees
of the central alley were putting forth their
tender leaves, and the orange trees were lining
the terrace which overlooks the Seine.   The
sun was shining full on the windows of the
palace, the whole façade was blazing with light.
What tragedies have been enacted since that
time in the ancient fortress of the French kings,
in sight of the green bowers—the fountains

and flowers of those beautiful gardens! What lives and what deaths, what crimes and what sorrows, have stamped bitter memories on their matchless loveliness! And still through every change of time and of doom, the horse-chestnuts put out their spiral blossoms and drop their shining fruit; and lovers whisper, and children play, and politicians talk, and men laugh and scheme in their shade, whether over the time-honoured dome of the old palace floats the spotless fleur-de-lis or the glorious tri-color.

Many a graceful picture of Boché or Vanloo might give an idea of the aspect of the Tuileries gardens on the day we are speaking of. Groups of fashionable loungers were sauntering up and down; the effect produced by their variegated dresses, their painted fans, their coloured parasols, and the gorgeous liveries of their servants, somewhat resembled that of the beds in the parterre, where tulips and sequinettes, anemones, crocuses and jonquils, were displaying their various hues in bright confusion. The reader of the foregoing pages may, perhaps, also picture to himself the mother and child,

who hastily withdrawing themselves from
the more fashionable part of the garden,
seated themselves on a bench in the
recess formed by the walls of the orangery.
There was certainly something very different
in their appearance from that of other people. They were not dressed in the height of
the fashion. In dress and in manner there
was a distinguished simplicity, a careless but
graceful negligence of effect, which would
have attracted the attention of a careful observer, but passed unobserved in a crowd.
Madame d'Auban's pale blue eyes were as
soft and lovely as ever, and her features
were still very beautiful; but during the last
few months she had grown to look much
older; a few grey hairs began to show themselves in her golden tresses. But as to Mina,
Wilhelmina as she was now oftener called,
there was no doubt as to her beauty. Nobody could have seen and not been struck
by it. If she had stood in the midst of the
fine ladies of the central alley, and chal-
lenged their notice, they might, indeed, have
lifted up their eyebrows with a supercilious
stare, and fluttering their fans declared, with
affected indifference, that the little creole was

tolerable enough ; but in their secret hearts each would have hoped that the eyes she herself wished to attract might never rest on the face of this young stranger. Though Mina was only in her thirteenth year, she looked fifteen or sixteen ; and her beauty was that of early girlhood rather than of childhood. The mind which spoke in her countenance was matured, also, beyond her age. The life she had led in her earlier years had strengthened and developed her frame, and the climate of Louisiana had prematurely hastened her growth. She was not as strong now as in her native Illinois ; her complexion was more delicate, and there was a darker shade under her eyes than that of the black eyelashes which fringed them. But many of the ladies of the court would have given the most costly pearl in their necklace, or the brightest stone in their coronals, for her dark blue and most expressive eyes—for her swanlike neck, or her features, chiselled like the fairest gem of Grecian art.

'I think papa is getting a great deal better now, dearest mother,' Mina said, as she unfolded a piece of embroidery, on which her slender fingers were soon busily employed.

'He is, indeed, much better. M. Lenoir's treatment has perfectly succeeded, and now he is of opinion that change of air will greatly contribute to his complete recovery.'

'Oh, how delightful! Then we shall leave Paris. Where shall we go?'

'My dear child, we do not mean to take you with us. Madame d'Orgeville has kindly invited you to spend the time of our absence with her daughters.'

Mina frowned, and, hiding her face in her hands, did not answer.

'You have many things to learn, my child, and you may never have such an opportunity again. I would not willingly cut short the time of your residence in Paris. The lessons you are taking now, from first-rate masters, are of the greatest advantage.'

Mina sighed. 'Could I not go to school in some convent?'

'Do you dislike Mesdemoiselles d'Orgeville?'

'I like Julie pretty well, and Oriane very much; but I cannot—indeed, mamma, I cannot—feel happy with them, as I used to do with Thérèse, Rose, and Agnes.'

There was a slight tone of irritation in Madame d'Auban's manner as she answered, ' That part of your life is past, Mina ; it is of no use to be always dwelling upon it, and nursing vain regrets. You are French, and it is not your destiny, my child, to live with Indians.'

' I cannot *feel* French, mother ! I cannot think or speak as they do. The girls here do not understand me. They do not care for the sky, or the trees, or the sunset clouds. Ontara and I used to talk of what the rivers whisper as they run by, and of the voices in the pine-trees. We knew what every flower said. I showed him one day a passion-flower, and I told him it was the flower of the Christians' prayer ; that the cross and the crown of thorns, the spear and the nails, were in its bosom, and that that was why I loved it so much ; and he pointed to a sun-flower, and said, " This is the flower of the Natchez' prayer. It worships the sun, as we do. Every day it turns to him as he sets the same look which it turned to him when he rose." '

'But, my Mina, Ontara is a heathen. How could you have felt so much sympathy with one who does not believe in Jesus Christ?'

Mina mused for a moment. She was putting to herself the same question. 'Mother, Ontara will be a Christian one day. He promised me never to part with his crucifix, and to say every day a prayer I taught him. Mother, Ontara will love our Lord one day; he loves the Great Spirit now much more than many of the French Christians do.'

'Do not say "the Great Spirit," Mina. You must leave off talking like the Indians.'

'I will say " the Good God," ' said Mina, gently. 'But, mother, some of the people here speak of the Supreme Being. Are they heathens?'

'Not much better than heathens, I am afraid,' said Madame d'Auban with a sigh. She looked anxiously at her daughter. A fear was perhaps crossing her mind lest her sweet wild-flower should lose its fragrance in the hothouse of a Parisian schoolroom.'

'Where are you and my father going?'
asked Mina, after a pause.

'To Brittany; he wishes to see his native
place again before leaving France, perhaps
for ever.'

Madame d'Auban did not add that this
was to be but the first step of a long journey,
the accomplishment of which was her long-
cherished hope.

'Mother, where is *your* native place?'
This was timidly said; Mina was conscious
that there was something mysterious in her
mother's fate. Many little circumstances had
led her to suspect it besides the prayers they
daily said in secret for her unknown brother.
She had never ventured before to put a direct
question to her on the subject. There was a
troubled look in her mother's face as she
answered—

'Your fate and mine, my daughter, may
be similar, I think, in one respect. Neither
of us will probably ever visit again the place
of our birth: but you may speak of yours; I
can never mention mine.'

Mina seized her mother's hand. 'I am so

sorry!' she said, tenderly kissing it. 'It is so sad never to speak of what we love!'

A sudden thought seemed to occur to Madame d'Auban. 'Mina,' she said, 'if in after years, perhaps when I am dead, it should ever come into your mind that, where so much concealment was necessary, there may have been guilt, remember what I now say to you. Never dream for a moment, my child, that there was aught to be ashamed of in your mother's life; keep in mind this solemn assurance, given at the eve of our first separation. You cannot understand its full meaning now, but you will hereafter. Your mother's history is an extraordinary one, but no disgrace is attached to it. These words must remain buried in your heart, my daughter. Question me not, nor others, on this subject; we will not revert to it again.'

Mina again kissed her mother, and then said, 'Is there the least chance, mamma, that the appointment papa hopes to obtain will be in the New France?'

'Not the least chance of it—banish all such hope from your mind, Mina. If a post

was offered him on the continent of America,
he would decline it. He does not wish, and
I would not for the world that he returned
to a country where he has suffered so much.
The effects of that terrible time are only now
disappearing. I always observed at New
Orleans that the sight of an Indian made him
shudder.'

The blood rushed to Mina's cheeks and
suffused her temples; her heart beat with
violence. 'And yet Ontara saved his life
and mine, and Pearl Feather died for us!'
she passionately exclaimed; and, rushing forward a little way beyond the bench, she
stood still, battling down the vehement feelings her mother's words had awakened. In
a few instants she returned, and, throwing
her arms round her mother's neck, whispered,
'Dearest, dearest papa, I know how much he
suffered, and he is so good; but, oh, mother,
some of my Indian brothers are good too!'

Just as the young girl was giving way to
this burst of feeling, the quiet corner where
her mother and herself were sitting was
invaded by a number of smartly-dressed persons, who formed themselves in a group just

opposite to them. They were discussing with great eagerness something that was going on or about to take place, and which evidently excited interest and amusement. In the centre of this assemblage stood a lady of unusual height, whose features were strikingly handsome. She was dressed in the extreme of fashion; spoke in a loud, ringing, but not unharmonious voice, and seemed to command the attention and admiration of the bystanders. The expression of her countenance varied every moment; sometimes wild merriment gleamed in her black eyes, and arch, mischievous smiles played on her lips, or a look of defiant resolution compressed them tightly together. At moments, a sweet and almost melancholy shade of thought overcast that sparkling brilliancy; she talked a great deal, and gesticulated incessantly.

'Does the great trial of strength really come off to-day?' asked one of the gentlemen who crowded round her. 'You have made a bold challenge, Mademoiselle, and I fear your backers will have to pay the costs.'

'Bah!' she said, laughing. 'Even defeat

in this case will be honourable. And so much the worse for those who have been rash enough to stake their fortunes on the strength of my wrist! A slender one, gentlemen,' she added, showing a well-shaped and very white hand.

'Does your antagonist furnish the plate ?'

'Of course he does.'

'My dear,' said one of the ladies, 'I am afraid you will be conquered. I know you bend five-franc pieces like wafers, but a silver plate! You have never yet attempted that.'

'I could not afford it.' There was a general burst of laughter.

'Mademoiselle grown economical! Wonders will never cease!'

'Perhaps not,' said the lady, and the thoughtful, mournful look came into her face, but in a second she was laughing again at her own thoughts, apparently. 'I could amuse you all very much,' she said, 'by relating my adventures since we last met here.'

'It has been reported that you had left Paris, but nobody could tell where you were gone,' said one of the gentlemen.

'I dare say not. Well, I went to the dull little capital of a foolish little kingdom. Guess now where I went.'

'I should never have guessed,' said another gentleman, 'that Mademoiselle Gaultier would have sought dulness under any form. There is no affinity between her and dulness.'

'I did not find Stutgard at all dull. On the contrary, the twenty-four hours I spent there were exceedingly lively.'

'And what in the name of patience took you there, my dear?' asked the same lady who had spoken before.

'Well, if you wish to hear the story, here it is. His Royal Highness of Wurtemburg and I were great friends all last winter. He is, as you know, a patron of the stage—writes plays himself—bad ones—but that is neither here nor there. He had often invited me to visit his duchy; so last week, as the weather was fine, and Paris not particularly amusing, I took it into my head to go. I travelled day and night, with only one servant. Oh, dear, what beautiful nights they were! I wonder if you Parisians have ever thought of looking at the stars? I assure you

it is very worth while. At the end of four
days I arrived at the König's Hof, and wrote
to my royal friend to announce my arrival.
He had the condescension to call upon me
on the same day, and was all bows and
smiles and compliments ; but when I spoke of
paying him my respects at the palace on the
morrow, I noticed a visible embarrassment on
the Grand-ducal countenance. He said there
was no occasion to fatigue myself so soon
after my journey—ah! ah! do I look like
a person easily fatigued?—and that he would
send his chamberlain the next day to inquire
after my health. And the chamberlain came,
and, what was more extraordinary, the chamberlain told the truth ! It appeared that his
Royal Highness, good soul, had betrayed im-
prudent marks of satisfaction on hearing of
my arrival, and had given orders that I should
be forthwith invited to dine at the palace.
But it was not to be. The noble and high
and mighty and virtuous Countess d'Ernsthumer, a Wurtemburgian — Madame de
Maintenon — a left-handed, morganatic sort
of divinity, presiding over the decorum and
morality of the pompous little court, had

decreed otherwise. She raised a tremendous
outcry, and protested against such an honour
being paid to Mademoiselle Gaultier, pre-
mière actrice du Théâtre Français. And the
veto took effect.'

' Too bad!' ' Too insolent!' ' Intolerable!'
' Impertinent!' exclaimed the listeners, in
different keys.

' What did you say to that wretched chamberlain ? '

' I asked if the excellent countess enjoyed
good health.'

' Good heavens ! my dear,' exclaimed one
of the ladies, ' you were not going to poison
her?'

' No; I am too much afraid of hell; and
besides, it would not have been half such fun
as what I did do.'

' And what on earth was that?' cried the
audience.

' Well, I took a drive the next day.'

' Is that all ? '

' I drove myself, of course, as I do here.
Mine host of the König's Hof, whose good
graces I had won by florins and civil speeches,
lent me a charming pair of unbroken horses,

which I ordered to be harnessed to a light phaeton. It had rained all night, and the ground was delightfully soft and muddy. My friend the chamberlain had kindly informed me at what hour I might have the pleasure of seeing all the beau monde of Stutgard parading up and down the promenade. Was not that a treat for a stranger from Paris? The Countess d'Ernsthumer, he said, always took a drive between one and two in her open carriage and four. I managed my wild steeds to perfection; we raced up and down the alleys, scattering mud in every direction. I kept them pretty well in hand till we came in sight of the morganatic equipage. 'Tis not to be described how frantic they then became—how they reared and plunged, and ended by running against its left wheel and sending it right over on its side—gently enough, too! The good German horses stood stock-still, and the ladies fell one upon another in the mud, like so many pillows in silk and muslin cases.'

'Well done!' 'Well done!' 'Bravo, Madlle. Gaultier!' re-echoed in the circle.

'Ay, but mind you, nobody cried "bravo" on the promenade at Stutgard (and the Germans can work themselves up into a fury if you give them time); so there was no time to lose, and I drove like the wind to my König's Hof, where a post-chaise and four was waiting for me. We flew rather than galloped to the frontier. The postboys had never before been promised so much Trinkgelt. Once on the French side of the river, I stood up in the carriage, shook my glove in defiance, and then flung it into the Rhine. In four more days and nights I travelled back to Paris, the only place fit for human beings to live in.'

'What did the Grand Duke think?' somebody said.

'Oh! I had a letter this morning describing the storm in a puddle which ensued. I was to have been thrown into prison. Ah! ah! The journey back was delightful. We had all sorts of adventures, and ran a thousand risks, Constant and I. We were nearly murdered in a cut-throat-looking inn.'

'Have you never known what it is to be frightened, Mademoiselle Gaultier?' a lady asked.

'I beg your pardon, Madame, I am terribly afraid of the least pain ; the prick of a needle makes me faint, and a hard bed cry. Mais que voulez-vous?—excitement is everything.'

Just then there was a stir amongst the bystanders. A man of high stature and noble appearance had joined the assemblage, and was standing opposite Mademoiselle Gaultier, with his back to Madame d'Auban and her daughter.

'Ah, Monsieur le Comte!' the actress gaily exclaimed, 'I was beginning to think you had forgotten my challenge.'

The person she thus addressed answered, with a smile : 'You are not content with one defeat, fair lady; you must needs seek another. So be it then. On the last occasion when we tried the strength of our wrists, you for-feited to me the rose which Zaïre had worn on the preceding evening. I am grown more ambitious now, and if I win I shall ask for the fellow of the glove which the free German Rhine is carrying to the sea.'

'Ah ! you have heard of my adventures, Monsieur le Comte ? Are you not afraid of measuring your strength with so malignant an enemy ?'

'Very much afraid,' answered the stranger, with a smile. 'But faint heart never won or vanquished fair lady ; so I must needs keep up my courage by all the inducements in my power. Here are two silver plates ; bent or unbent, they remain yours after the trial ; and if I win, then I claim the champion's glove.'

'Very well,' said Mademoiselle Gaultier. 'Give me a plate.'

It was handed to her. She took it up with a half-confident, half-doubtful look, colouring with eagerness, and smiling as if anticipating a triumph. Then laying it down again, she began by bending with her fingers, slender and thin, but as strong as steel, a five-franc piece, which she rolled as if it had been a wafer. Everybody applauded.

'Now for the great attempt!' she said ; and the eyes of all present were fixed upon her as she again took up the silver plate.

Madame d'Auban and Mina were watching her like the rest. There was something

irresistibly attractive in the good-humoured
wilfulness of her handsome face.

'Nobody has ever conquered me,' she
said, overlooking, with feminine inconsist-
ency, her recent defeat.

When a woman wills something, and that
something is a triumph of some kind, how
resolved she is upon it! The colour deepened
visibly under the rouge on her cheeks. She
bent the whole strength of her fingers, of her
arm, of her whole frame on the plate, which
would not yield to that desperate pressure.
Her lips were firmly and tightly compressed;
the veins in her forehead swelled. She
turned pale with the prolonged effort.
'Allons! I am beat,' she cried, vexed and
yet laughing. 'I don't believe you can bend
it, Monsieur le Comte.'

The stranger bowed, took it up, and with
a scarcely perceptible effort rolled it up like
a piece of parchment.

'Bravo!' exclaimed the lady, with frank
good humour, and pulling off her glove she
presented it to her antagonist with a graceful
curtsey. 'To have entered the lists with such
an adversary is in itself an honour, and to be

defeated by him more glorious than to conquer a meaner foe. And yet,' she added, laughing, ' it is pitiful not to be able any more to boast that what anybody else has done one can also do.'

Her cortége accompanied her as she moved away, and no one remained in that part of the garden but Madame d'Auban and Mina and Madlle. Gautlier's antagonist, who suddenly turned round and sat down at the farthest end of the bench where they were seated. He took out a parcel of letters from his pocket and began to read them, without paying any attention to his neighbours. Mina had been much amused with the scene she had witnessed.

' Is not that gentleman wonderfully strong, mamma ? ' she said in French.

' Speak German,' whispered her mother, glancing at the stranger.

' The lady is also very strong,' Mina said in that language, ' and she is very handsome too. Do you think she looks good, mamma ? '

The gentleman at the end of the bench evidently understood German, for he turned round, amused at Mina's question, and looked

at her with curiosity first and then with un-
mistakable admiration. But he soon resumed
his reading.

'I think her manners are too bold, but
there is something prepossessing in her countenance,' was Madame d'Auban's answer to
her daughter's remark.

'Yes, mamma; I see what you mean about
her being too bold, but I am glad you like
her face. I do.'

'She is an actress—not a person in
society.'

'An actress! I wonder if she acts as well
as Pouponne?'

'Who is Pouponne, my dear?'

'Madame de Simiane's grand-daughter,
mamma. She came the other day to see Julie
and Oriane, and she told us that at her school
they were going to act Athalie, and that she
was going to be the Queen. M. d'Héricourt
had been teaching her when to stand and
to sit down, and to put out her hand, and to
look up to heaven. She repeated to us her
part; you can't think how well she did it,
mamma; especially that bit when Athalie
says:—

" Où serais-je aujourd'hui si domptant ma faiblesse
Je n'eusse d'une mère étouffé la tendresse ? " '

' Hush, darling ! ' said her mother, and an expression of pain passed over her face.

Mina perceived it, and, hastening to change the subject, exclaimed, ' I wish I was a queen! Not a make-believe one, but a queen in good earnest.'

' What can make you wish for such a fate, Mina ? '

' I would then fit out an immense ship and return to America, and on the top of the hill where Eagle-eye used to carry me I would build a cathedral as large as Nôtre Dame, which would be the wonder of the New World.'

' Do you fancy that kings and queens are free agents, my child; or, that they are happier than other people ? '

' Everybody says—happy as a king or a queen. Julie says, she should be as happy as a queen if she married somebody about the Court, and was invited to Marly.'

' Those who use that form of speech have never known what anguish often wrings the hearts of those they foolishly envy.'

Mina laid her head in a caressing manner against her mother's shoulder, and looking up into her face said, 'But how do you know what they suffer, sweetest mother? You have never lived in a palace.'

Madame d'Auban pushed back the curls from her daughter's forehead, and, pressing her lips upon it, murmured, 'Take my word for it, Mina, there is sometimes no slavery more galling than that of royalty, and no more melancholy prison than a palace. The hardest of all chains are often invisible; and many a heart breaks in silence on or near a throne.'

These last words, uttered with some emotion, and in a rather louder voice than that in which Madame d'Auban had hitherto spoken, caused the stranger, who had now finished reading his letters, to bend forward and endeavour to catch a glimpse of her face; but, not succeeding, he collected his papers and walked away. As he passed before Madame d'Auban he looked hard at her, and in a few minutes turned back again and fixed his eyes earnestly upon her. She remarked it, and for the first time she also caught sight of his features, and felt at once that they were not unknown to her.

'Put up your work, darling,' she hurriedly said. 'It is time to go.'

'Oh, do let us stay a little longer, dearest mamma! It is so pleasant now under the trees.'

'No, no; make haste, Mina.'

For the third time the stranger turned back, and this time he stopped opposite to them. Madame d'Auban's eyes met his eager glance, and every trace of colour vanished from her cheek. She remained motionless and cold as any of the stone statues about her. The stranger pronounced a single word, 'Madame!' There was wonder, respect, and a tacit enquiry in the tone with which it was uttered. In the ears of her to whom it was addressed, it sounded like a voice from another world; for that stranger and herself had been friends in early youth—almost like a brother had that man been to her; and at sight of him thoughts of her family, and home, and old associations were rushing upon her with indescribable might.

'The Comte de Saxe,' she murmured.

The name died away on her lips, but she could not repress the choking and blinding tears which would flow in spite of all her efforts.'

'Dear companion of my childhood,' the Count began, in a low and rapid tone—'friend of my earlier days, do my senses beguile me, or do I, indeed, behold you again? Oh, madame, what does this mean? What miracle has raised you from an untimely grave? For God's sake, explain to me this mystery!'

Madame d'Auban made a strong effort to rise, and leaning on Mina she turned away. 'It is a mistake,' she faintly said, and tried to walk on. But the Count seized her hand and exclaimed—

'It is your voice, as well as your face! It is yourself! You cannot deceive me!'

'Let go my mother's hand,' cried Mina, with the air of a young chieftainess. 'You make her weep. Begone!'

Without heeding her, the Count continued —'Good God! madame! cannot you trust me? Have you the heart to treat me as a stranger?'

She had struggled for composure, and partly regained it. A thousand rapid thoughts and fears had passed through her mind. In those days of irresponsible power in sovereigns, and with the strong abhorrence of mesalliances in royal families, there was more ground for her apprehensions than can be easily conceived in the present day. In a steadier tone she said—'This is some singular misapprehension, sir. I have been ill, and was overcome by the suddenness of your strange address. Some accidental resemblance, I suppose——'

'Resemblance!' cried the Count, impatiently. 'But be it so, madame, if such is your will. My respect is as unbounded as my attachment is profound. Far be it from me to intrude upon you. Your simplest wish is as much a law to me now as when at your father's——'

'Hush! for God's sake hush!' The words burst from Madame d'Auban's lips, as she glanced at Mina, and, before she had time to recall them, she felt that she had tacitly acknowledged what she meant to hide. A crimson hue overspread her face.

'Your daughter?' said the Count de Saxe, glancing admiringly at Mina, who was frowning at the audacious stranger. 'And her name is——?'

'Wilhelmina d'Auban,' cried the young girl; 'and I wish some of my brave Indians were here to drive you away.'

'Ah! madame, we have both mourned,' said the Count—'both wept over the loss of another Wilhelmina.'

Madame d'Auban burst into tears.

'Do sit down again,' cried the Count de Saxe; and she did do, for her limbs were trembling, so that she could hardly stand. He stood for a moment gazing upon her with an expression in which anxiety, curiosity, and sympathy were all combined. Mina looked from one to the other with a perplexed and anxious countenance. At last, in a tone of deep feeling, he said—'I know not whether to go or to stay. I scarcely know how to address you, madame. Would to God you would speak to me one word only! Tell me, I am not mad!'

Madame d'Auban raised her tearful eyes, and looked at him with that peculiar expression which had made the Princess Charlotte of Wolfenbuttel the object of his boyish worship, and she answered in a tremulous voice, 'She whom you think you see is indeed dead—dead to kindred, to friends, to that world in which she once lived. Do not disturb the peace of her grave. Forget the stranger you have met to-day.'

'Could I ever think of *you* as a stranger?'

'Think of me as you please! But, oh, M. de Saxe, be kind, be generous, and do not by a fatal curiosity ruin happiness which hangs on a thread!'

'You are happy, then?'

Madame d'Auban glanced at her daughter, and bowed her head in assent.

'Heaven forbid I should cause you a moment's uneasiness! I will, of course, forbear from any enquiries that may pain you or endanger your peace; but may I not come and see you? Will you not give me the explanation of what an hour hence will seem to me an incredible dream?'

'M. de Saxe, if you will give me your word of honour that you will be silent as the grave,

ay, as the grave itself, as to this meeting,
I will write in three months' time, and explain to you this mystery. I may then have
a favour to ask of you.'

'I promise—I swear,' eagerly cried the
Comte de Saxe ; 'but if at the end of three
months I do not hear from you, I shall
think it my duty to inform the King, my
master, of your existence ?'

' In three months ? So be it. But if I live,
you will hear from me before that time.
You promise that you will not follow me
now, or seek to discover my abode ?'

' I promise,' answered the Count. ' But if
during that interval you should need the aid
of a strong arm and a devoted heart, think,
madame, of Maurice of Saxony. I suppose I
must not ask for one word of kind farewell ?'

Madame d'Auban held out her hand, which
he kissed with profound respect. ' Farewell,
and Heaven bless you, Maurice,' she said in
a trembling voice.

When the mother and daughter had disappeared, the Comte de Saxe stood some
time in the same place, musing on this

extraordinary meeting with one whom for years he had thought of as dead. 'If I am not more mad than any madman in Bicêtre,' he inwardly exclaimed, ' truth is stranger than the wildest fiction.'

END OF THE SECOND VOLUME.

www.ingramcontent.com/pod-product-compliance
Lightning Source LLC
Chambersburg PA
CBHW030638030726
47497CB00006B/1839